This Business of the Flesh

"C. Kubasta's *This Business of the Flesh* is so compelling and engaging that I read it straight through. You don't have to be a dog person to appreciate how much she knows about dogs, because she knows plenty about the human species too, and she certainly knows how to write about the human body and its desires. Her novel is smart and funny and irresistible, with plenty of room for all kinds of life-forms."

> — Valerie Sayers, author of *The Powers* and *Brain Fever*

"*This Business of the Flesh* is a noble, quiet, and ultimately graceful novel populated by a chorus of believable, flawed, and charming characters - a few of them of the animal-variety. A jaunty, heartfelt, and occasionally sexy book that demonstrates the unlikely ways in which we discover salvation and forgiveness."

> — Nickolas Butler, internationally best-selling author of *Shotgun Lovesongs, Beneath the Bonfire*, and *The Hearts of Men*

"In *This Business of the Flesh*, Kubasta provides sharp insight into complex family dynamics and the interconnected relationships in a small town, moving effortlessly among characters, wrestling with stories of class, environmental concerns, and the nature of a happy life. A story of small-town America told with refreshing dignity and respect for its people and their stories, Kubasta introduces a cast you'll be happy to spend time with. You'll marvel at how she so quickly brings these characters and the lives they inhabit to life."

> — Chrissy Kolaya, author of *Charmed Particles: a novel and Any Anxious Body: poems*

"Achingly raw and exquisitely poetic, *This Business of the Flesh* is a meditation on the blood and bones of our existence; fierce and tender Americana."

> — Christie Perfetti Williams, writer, producer Carnival Girls Productions

This Business of the Flesh

C. Kubasta

Apprentice House Press
Loyola University Maryland

First Edition

Casebound ISBN: 978-1-62720-187-2
Paperback ISBN: 978-1-62720-188-9
Ebook ISBN: 978-1-62720-189-6

Printed in the United States of America

Design by Mary-Elizabeth Esquibel
Marketing by Zhi Yi Yeo
Development by Abigail Zonarich

Cover photo by Stephen Matthew Milligan, licensed under the Creative Commons Attribution-Share Alike 3.0 Unported license.

Published by Apprentice House

Apprentice House Press
Loyola University Maryland

Apprentice House
Loyola University Maryland
4501 N. Charles Street
Baltimore, MD 21210
410.617.5265 • 410.617.2198 (fax)
www.ApprenticeHouse.com
info@ApprenticeHouse.com

In memory of Harry, who first &
always encouraged me to write

Contents

Part One: June 1

    The Dogs 3

    Tracy.. 15

    Lucy... 25

    Fences 39

Part Two: July 49

    Appointments 51

    Round Two 61

    Sarah.. 69

    Carla... 75

    Kindness 87

    Meetings 91

Part Three: August 99

    Greg... 101

    Conversation 107

    The Lake 115

    What Needed to be Done 121

    3:12 125

    Might as Well 133

    Restraint 143

    Epilogue: The Wedding............................... 149

Acknowledgements... 153

About the Author 155

Part One: June

The Dogs

Tracy and her father followed the man from downtown onto Foothills Road, then onto a tracery of back roads, some paved, some not. Sam had one hundred fifty acres that he mostly used for hunting. He lived nearer to Lewiston, and told them they could have flown into there, although the tickets are more expensive. There were two cabins on the property; one he used, and the one he had rented to Aaron. He'd met Aaron about eight months ago, in a local bar, and he'd seemed like a nice guy. Sam had been looking for a caretaker, as he'd had some vandalism, and had been worried about squatters. Aaron paid rent up front (cash), agreed to clean up some brush, walk the woods, and keep an eye out for trespassers. Sam thought Aaron was maybe one of those hippie types, those live-off-the-grid fantasy guys, but they didn't have any problems until the dogs. And even that ended up being all right in the end.

After they turned onto the dirt driveway of Sam's land, he'd parked, suggested they leave the rental car and join him in his truck. Her father looked uncomfortable, but agreed. Tracy sat in the middle, her father against the door. He pressed his body away from hers, avoiding the discomfort of another person's shoulder and elbow jostling against his in the cab as it bucked over ruts.

Sam told them the story of the dogs. He'd come out in March, when the snow began to melt, pulled up to Aaron's cabin, and the pits had run out, all teeth. Aaron had run out right after.

"Lucky, I already had the safety off my gun."

Tracy bristled. Even though she'd grown up in the land of deer hunting, and now conceal-carry, she'd never felt comfortable with this easy talk of guns.

"The silver one must have just had a litter. Her ti—well, you could tell she'd just had 'em. And the red one, those always look kind of spooky," Sam continued, a low chuckle.

"Pits?" Her father perked up. "Pit bulls? Aren't those dogs vicious?"

"Pit bulls have a bad reputation Dad, but they aren't all bad," Tracy answered, although she was starting to feel unsure herself. She had read this somewhere about pit bulls, but she'd never really spent any time with those types of dogs – with any dogs really.

"Tracy, we will not," he enunciated each syllable, "be bringing any pit bulls home."

"Well, sir," Sam responded and she appreciated the "sir." He must have heard the consonants. "They're really sweet dogs. But I must admit, I'm partial to Stella."

After about five more minutes of driving, they pulled up to the cabin. Her father said he'd wait in the car, so Tracy slid out the driver's side after Sam. The minute they opened the door the pits were all over them. One was silver-grey and one was red, with freckles. They wagged their tails so hard it was as if they had no spines, their bodies curving into *c's*, then curving back again, as they jumped and licked and pranced, their nails clicking on the wide plank floors. After a few seconds of greeting, Sam yelled "Out!" and the dogs scampered out the door, racing around the yard.

In the far corner of the room, Tracy could see a third dog. It raised itself from a bed on the floor, heavy-boned and muscled, the head square and red, surrounded by jowls. Two strings of drool seemed to be attached to the floor, and as it slowly stood, the strings stretched like elastic until they snapped. The dog locked its front legs, lowered its head, and stared at Tracy.

"Stella warms up a little more slowly," Sam said. "What you're going to want to do is sit in that chair there." He motioned to a green chair right beside the door. "She's going to come and sniff you and you're going to pretend there's no dog in the room. Don't pet her or talk to her or make eye contact." Tracy sat.

Stella moved slowly. She walked forward, almost a saunter, and buried her large head between Sam's legs. She made rhythmic grunting noises, a dog purr. He massaged the rolls of skin around her neck, lowering his face to her back. "Oh Stella." He said "Stella," doing some impression of Brando as Stanley Kowalski. After a few seconds, Stella backed up, slowly still, and then moved toward the door, stopping alongside Tracy. The dog sniffed her backside where she was hunched forward, away from the back of the chair.

"You OK?" Sam asked.

"Am I?"

"Sure. Stella just has to get to know people a little. She's a discerning girl." He smiled. "Just keep talking to me."

"How long did it take her to get to know you?"

"By my second visit, I was all right. But she can be pretty intimidating at first. I thought you might remind her of Aaron." Tracy's eyes welled up; just then Stella snorted and Tracy jumped.

"Easy, girl," Sam said, but Tracy didn't know if he was talking to the dog or to her.

Stella continued out the door, joined the other dogs sitting alongside the truck, staring up at the passenger window where Tracy could see the whites of her father's eyes.

Tracy's brother Aaron had been living in Idaho, in that small cabin, with those dogs. The man he was renting a cabin from had found him, and his driver's license (with his parent's address), and had contacted the local police in Wisconsin. They'd gone to his parent's house, knowing this wasn't the kind of news to be delivered over the phone. After a flurry of phone calls between the authorities in some place called Moscow, the local funeral home, Tracy, and the family attorney, arrangements had been made. Aaron was cremated, his cremains flown home. When Aaron's father talked to the landowner, he'd said he didn't want anything, to dispose of Aaron's possessions. Tracy and her mother had been in the kitchen, listening.

"Wait, Dad..." Tracy had said.

"Well, sir," said the man on the phone, "it's not that simple."

"Why not?"

"I'm not comfortable with going through your son's things, for one," he said.

"I give you permission." Tracy was crossing the kitchen to where her father was standing in the living room, looking out the bay window at the lake.

"Dad," she said, tersely, eyes still red-rimmed. He turned to her.

"And there's also the dogs to be seen to..."

"The dogs?" Her father asked as Tracy took the phone.

The man continued. "Aaron had three dogs, real sweet, and I don't want to..." The man on the other end was still talking, his voice tinny.

"This is Tracy, Aaron's sister," she interrupted.

"I'm sorry for your loss, Miss."

"Umm, thank you. Three dogs?"

"Yeah, well, I wasn't real happy when I found out about the dogs at first, but they're good dogs, and I don't want to send them to the pound. Two are pits and they'd probably be euthanized, but Miss, when I found your brother, the dogs were sleeping with him, all cuddled up, kind of guarding him. He really loved those dogs."

"Oh."

"And Miss, Aaron had a real nice place here, and I think his family might like to have some of his things... I wouldn't feel right about just throwing things away."

"Oh," Tracy said. "Well, I guess we should come out then."

"I really think you should."

Tracy's parents were well off, but in their small town they were downright rich. Most of the people in their tax bracket only came up in the summer, to their homes on the lake, and lived the rest of the year in Milwaukee or Chicago. For some reason, Tracy and Aaron and their mother lived there all year long. Their small-town school was big by the standards of rural counties, a consolidated school district with class sizes that hovered around a hundred students. Even taking out Tracy and Aaron and a few other wealthier kids, the class distinctions were noticeable. There were the farm kids who often were late for first period, and smelled of manure and milk replacer. There were the poorer town kids, most of whom would scrape through to graduation, but definitely would not be going to college, or even tech school, instead taking jobs right away at the foundry or the processing plant. A few would just disappear. There were the migrant kids who came and went who nobody seemed to get to know. There were the girls, a few each year, beginning in eighth grade, who got pregnant and disappeared forever, so the school started offering an elective in high school called "Parenting" that raised a few eyebrows and caused some dissension at a school board meeting, resulting in a debate about dropping sex education altogether, one argument being that the school's discussion of sex being a thing was encouraging teenagers to engage in it. Most of the town kids would go to a technical college, or a state school, either the two-year colleges, earning associate's degrees or eventually transferring to one of the state universities for bachelor's degrees in "something practical." A few students would go out of state, but to their church-sponsored school. Both Aaron and Tracy tried to fit in, doing the things their classmates did – yearbook, forensics, track – but always knowing in some way that they were different as well. Local news about the muffler plant closing down didn't weigh heavily on their mother and father, didn't sit a place at the dinner table, shushing everyone to silence. So when Tracy returned home after college and started dating Greg, a local boy from a local family, her father had called to tell her he was "disappointed."

"Are you marrying this 'Greg'?" her father had asked at the end of one of their already stilted phone calls.

Greg had not gone to college. But he could build anything, from the restored car in his garage to the hay bale house he'd started for the two of them. He was a forager, knew how to locate hen o' the woods mushrooms, morels, and fiddleheads. If she woke to a cold bed in the morning, she knew he'd be back with breakfast – maybe fresh bluegills, or eggs from their chickens. After they'd been dating just a few weeks, he'd asked her to "share his life." Those were his exact words. So when Tracy's father asked, she said "No," and "His name is just Greg, Dad – no need for the extra flourish."

Tracy had begun disappointing her father when she'd majored in business and minored in communication, definitely a "practical choice," like the kids who didn't know they could dream bigger: a pre-major that necessitated graduate school and ensured more years of study, a hefty starting salary and the prestige of certain letters that automatically attach to a person's last name. She'd continued disappointing him when she'd decided not to go to graduate school and returned home. Greg was probably the last straw, but since then Tracy and her father had settled into a kind of truce. Although they lived within a few miles of each other, they kept their contact to a minimum: major holidays and birthdays. She didn't bring Greg around; they didn't talk about anything beyond the perfunctory niceties. She maintained access to her gifted money, checked on Aaron, and reported back what she could without upsetting her mother too much.

Until about a year ago, the news on Aaron was disappointingly the same. His depression was clinical and constant. When he was under a doctor's care, there would be some hope, some new combination of pharmaceuticals that would improve his affect, and even allow him to take some joy in interacting with his sister from time to time. But often the lifting that came with this relief from the worst symptoms would also lead to new energies that would turn self-destructive. He had been hospitalized for suicide attempts several times since his one semester of college. Since that first terrible phone call, there had been more, almost a routine. Despite Tracy's mother's busyness with all things domestic, she rarely answered the phone anymore – certainly a learned behavior. Aaron's college roommate had been so kind to him that they hadn't known how bad it had been before that first phone call. How he had re-arranged his class schedule to check in on Aaron several times a day, stayed weekends at the dorm arranging movie fests and study sessions, even making an anonymous report to the dean of students.

When Tracy drove with her father to pick Aaron up from the university, and her father was loading the car, the roommate had taken Tracy aside and explained the details. Tracy had recognized her old fears. This young man, only eighteen himself, had become Aaron's keeper. After their first two weeks of college, the old Aaron had returned: the old Aaron who rarely stirred from his bed; whose clothing and pajamas became indistinguishable, sleep-creased, and stiffened; whose only activity seemed to be silent surfing online, an eerie echo of taps on keys and mouse clicks; whose communication became reduced to small grunts, and even that without eye contact. The roommate had tried everything he could think of – taking Aaron out to dinner, to walk State Street, to parties, introducing him to girls who liked quiet, dark types who themselves tried to draw Aaron out. Nothing worked and he felt like a failure, just like Tracy felt like a failure. And Tracy, who was not given to hugs, certainly not to strangers, hugged this stranger and said *thank you*, said *it's not your fault, there's nothing you could do*, said *we appreciate your help*, and meant it. Tracy and her father loaded the car at the dorm and after Aaron was released from the psych ward, took him home. Aaron sat in the backseat, staring out the window the whole way, worrying the hospital bracelet on his arm, the skin of his wrist winter-pallor white and flaking.

Aaron's illness seemed to embarrass his parents, their natural reserve deepening and steeping. And Aaron was irritated by his parents, by their embarrassment or concern, whichever it was. He moved out one weekday afternoon when his father was at work and his mother was running errands. Tracy then became the conduit of information, checking on Aaron when she could locate him through his ever-changing addresses and phone numbers. His trust fund took care of expenses and his doctors had her number; she was his contact-in-case-of-emergency person. This went on for years: the years that stretched between Tracy's return, the years of Greg; a tumble of years, all sameness with occasional chasms of deep worry or guarded hope. But Aaron made a large cash withdrawal about a year ago and disappeared for good. When she couldn't locate him, she called her father. He seemed to take the news in stride. At the end of the call, he asked, perfunctorily, "How's Greg?"

She hadn't told him about their break up, or the dissolution of their business, both over a year old. Hearing her father say her ex's name, after years of him never bothering to ask, made her start to tingle and itch, like all of her was the sensitive skin on her forearms getting too close to a tomato plant. Somehow she thought he would have heard about it, or at least noticed that the trucks with their business name were no longer seen around town.

"We broke up Dad," she said, swallowing.

"Oh. Probably for the best," he said. "Let me know if you find anything out about your brother," and he hung up.

In preparation for the flight into Spokane and the rental car journey to Moscow, Tracy packed several books (a couple of novels and a how-to home repair book) to use as armor against her father and conversation. She imagined him doing the same, carefully selecting various work projects – some that required close concentration, some that required cursory glances – to keep him insulated from whatever he didn't want to see, or talk about – tools of useful distraction. In this, as in other ways, Tracy and her father were similar. This trip, to discover and collect the last year of her brother's life, would be the most concentrated time she and her father had ever spent together. So many things to not talk about.

Growing up, she only sometimes found it strange that she and Aaron and her mother were a family of three most of the time. When her father was working full-time, he'd only come up from Milwaukee on the weekends. In the winter, when the weather was unpredictable, he'd stay in the city and it would be just the three of them for weeks. She and her brother didn't miss him; she never knew if her mother did. When she became a teenager, she'd occasionally go for a weekend in the city, stay in the apartment downtown where she could go to the art museum or see a concert. She could bring friends if she wanted to and her father left her alone as much as she wanted, leaving her a number for the car service, a couple credit cards, and a stack of cash. Her hometown friends thought this was "very cool" but were intimidated by the city, unless they could watch the nighttime streets from behind the tinted windows of the rented car. She and Aaron would have fun when they went together, if he was in the mood to go out – to the Rave to see bands on their Midwestern tours, or visit the ethnic fairs, or Summerfest.

The first two years of high school, Tracy realized, was when she'd lost track of Aaron, distracted by her new freedoms and her new friends. That was when she'd started having the dreams – long before any of them knew consciously that he was in danger. The dreams were always the same: someone was hurting Aaron. She never saw who it was, but the danger was real, and advancing and meant to cause bodily harm to her brother – to torture and kill him. In the most common dream, Aaron is an infant and she has to carry him around. The danger is the kind of killer who enjoys exacting pain before delivering death. The landscape is flat, mostly sand and scrub. She stumbles, carrying infant-Aaron, and tries to outrun the killer. She swaddles and wraps him in bandages, but blood is seeping through from the wounds. The killer has cut and torn and stripped his skin off, but infant-Aaron doesn't scream in pain anymore, he whimpers. She knows she can't outrun the killer forever and she knows she needs to get help. Infant-Aaron is heavy; he's weighing her down. She sets him down and runs for help. She digs a hole in the ground and hides him in it, runs as fast as she can, hoping he'll be quiet and she'll get back in time. She always woke up before she could get back to help him.

She always woke up before she could get back. Night after night she'd have some variation of this dream. She'd have to go for help, his poor body hurt and broken. She couldn't save him herself. And in the morning, she'd be sitting across the breakfast table from him, eating her hot oatmeal or eggs, readying for high school while he readied for middle school across town; their mother in the kitchen, their father in Milwaukee in his apartment.

Now she and her father were on a plane, both of them with something open on their laps, to protect them from each other. They were going to where Aaron had lived and died, not knowing what they are going to find.

Her father refused to come into the cabin until the dogs were locked in the back bedroom. Sam was right about Stella: as long as Tracy ignored her, Stella did the same. She really was an impressive animal – loose flesh collected around her neck and chest and when she ran it swayed with her gait; her eyes were amber, her paws were huge. With the dogs locked up, she and her father inspected the cabin. Well, she did. It was one large room, a connected living room and kitchenette, furnished with a couch, the green greeting chair, and a small desk. There was the small bedroom, and a bathroom with a stand-up shower, and a composting toilet. Her father wrinkled his nose. He gave the space and Aaron's belongings a cursory glance, then walked outside where Sam had gone to give them privacy.

Once Tracy started looking, she couldn't stop. There was a small wood-stove and a stack of perfectly split and stacked logs. There were three cast iron skillets, well-seasoned and well-used. There was an orderly root cellar. Trays of started seedlings were on the window sills, mostly vegetables, now parched and drooping. There were the dogs' bowls. There were jars of saffron and turmeric and arctic root. There were shelves with novels and poetry and self-help books; dog books, *The Monks of New Skete*, Patricia McConnell. There was a light table. And there was what was missing: his pharmaceuticals, his videogames, anything wired. He was trying to get better. Aaron had withdrawn here to get better and return to himself, maybe to return to her.

And there would be Sam's stories about Aaron, stories of an Aaron she didn't know: the Aaron who helped him fell trees and clear a space for a new pole building; the Aaron who joined him and his hunting buddies for beers; the Aaron who could tell a great story, entertaining everyone; the Aaron who rescued the silver bitch from the roadside where she'd been dumped, her puppies drowned; the red bait dog and Stella, returned six times to the shelter, scheduled for euthanasia.

In the end, she and her father argued. He took the rental car and flew back. She stayed for a week at the cabin, going through Aaron's things, packing what she wanted, discarding what she didn't. It took Stella about four days to warm to her, but they co-existed in the small space with no animosity. She fed the dogs, let them out, took them for walks in the woods. The pits, who she took to calling Smoke and Red (Sam didn't think they really had names), loved her immediately, curling up on either side of her on the couch when she read her books, and when she'd finished those, started on Aaron's bookshelves. She found his journals but boxed those up right away, not yet ready to read them.

Sam was staying at his cabin for the week too. He stopped over early afternoon on her second day there to check in on her. He was probably a few years younger than her father, but seemed quite a bit younger, rangy and lean, with a weather-beaten face that was very sexy. She was glad to see him, asked him back for dinner that night.

"Are you sure? I mean, I don't want to intrude."

"Please. You can help convince Stella I'm OK," she smiled. The big dog was leaning against the tall grey-haired man, staring up at him lovelorn. "She probably feels doubly abandoned."

He arrived that night with a six-pack and a pizza, fired up the grill and showed her how to grill frozen pizza when there's no oven, doctoring it with a few of Aaron's leftover provisions – some mushrooms he reconstituted in water, the dried basil leaves that were tied up in the eaves. They sat around the fire ring and he told her how he had found Aaron, how he thought that Aaron had probably arranged it that way, not wanting the dogs to suffer. He'd likely taken the pills the day before. The dogs' food and water bowls were full, but they hadn't touched them. When he knocked and yelled and Aaron didn't answer, but the dogs were whining, he knew something wasn't right, so he'd walked in. The pits were together on the couch, looking shell-shocked. But Stella was curled around Aaron's body, so that his head was cradled on her big belly. She was shaking and lying in a puddle of her own drool.

Tracy was glad dusk had fallen but thought that her wet eyes were probably still visible in the firelight. She let her bangs, which were getting a bit long, fall into her eyes.

"You OK, Tracy? I'm sorry–I shouldn't be telling you this..."

"No, it's OK. I want to know. Keep going."

Maybe Stella had curled around him after he was gone. Maybe he'd lain down with her. Either way, that's how Sam had found him. He said Stella let out the most plaintive sound he'd ever heard a dog make, worse than the pain he'd heard his own dog cry when it got hit by a car, almost wrenching its leg clear off.

Sam came out a few more times to help her load boxes, light a bonfire, and move the heavy things. He drove her into town to rent a panel van and buy a double mattress for the back, to haul the dogs home with her. When she told him she was taking all three of them, that she was keeping them, he hugged her hard. When he pulled away, his eyes were wet, and he kissed her on the mouth. She'd mostly decided that night, after Sam told her about Stella holding Aaron. She figured they'd get used to each other. But two days later, she woke in the morning, and it hit her all over again that her brother was dead, that there was nothing she could do, that she'd never be able to go back for him, to protect him, to save him from the danger. She started crying, quietly at first, then louder, and pretty soon she was sobbing full-throated into her pillow like a child with no control over anything.

She felt her. The bed sunk down a few inches and she froze. It was Stella. The pits didn't come on the bed, they slept on the couch for naps and all night long. The dog's big paws rocked the mattress, like a kayak steered crosswise in a motorboat's wake. She circled twice then dropped to her belly, her spine lined up perfectly with Tracy's, her head on the pillow facing the other way. They were mirror images of each other. Tracy whimpered. Stella sighed heavily, and Tracy could hear the air escape her meaty jowls, the *phfft* as they flapped softly together.

Tracy

Tracy had been home all of six minutes before she heard Deb coming up the back steps. "Yoo hoo," Deb called, opening the screen door. Tracy rushed to the door, trying to block the dogs, but Smoke and Red wriggled over and under her bent knees. Deb froze, holding rubber-banded bundles of mail in her arms, her sun hat askew, her cheeks already red from a few glasses of wine. Her mouth was open in a wide O.

"Smoke! Red!" Tracy yelled at the dogs, who continued to squirm around Deb's locked knees. Tracy let the screen door slam, where slow Stella stood, just on the other side, very still. "Deb, it's OK, they're very friendly," and she could see Deb relax, take in the wagging tails whipping around her exposed calves in her peasant skirt, her sneakers, and short athletic socks. Deb collapsed into the folding lawn chair on the brick patio and took a deep breath. The van was in the driveway, the engine ticking as it cooled, the back doors wide open. Tracy had just had time to go to the bathroom and let the dogs inside when she heard her neighbor's voice entering the house. The dogs had six hours of energy they were quickly releasing onto hapless Deb, triply surprised.

"They do look friendly enough," she said, setting the mail down and putting her hands out to be sniffed. The two pits took to enthusiastically licking the proffered hands, wriggling their dog dance around the sitting woman. "These two anyway," Deb continued, looking toward the door. "Not so sure about that one."

"That's Stella," Tracy said, "and she's a little tougher to get to know. Discerning, you might say," and as Tracy said it, she thought of how Sam had described Stella to her. The dog remained stock still behind the screen, all muzzle, slightly blued by the wire mesh, blowing a bubble of drool out of one jowl. Her eyes concentrated on Deb, flicking every so often back to Tracy.

"Well she can keep 'discerning' me from behind that door."

Tracy ignored that. There'd be plenty of time to introduce Deb and Stella. Over the nearly two weeks she'd been gone, everything had grown, a rush of summer. The ferns were full, waist-high, wafting their damp smell over the driveway. The grass was long enough to warrant a visit from the town code inspector, if a busybody neighbor bothered to alert them. Along the house, it was impossible to distinguish what was planted and intentional from what was weed, volunteer and intrusive.

"Sorry, Trace. You just got home. Let's talk tomorrow. I just wanted to bring you your mail." She pointed to the stacks on the table, accumulated over the nearly two weeks she'd been gone. "And tell you you had a visitor. Sexy beardy," and she winked.

Deborah was a remarkable woman. She had two pastimes. The first was known to everyone in town – shameless flirtation with any man between nineteen and ninety. She appraised them, gave them jaunty monikers, and could somehow tell them apart and remember their stats like they were her own private baseball team. Her style of flirtation was the double entendre and the innuendo. Her creativity was boundless. She exercised her wits with delivery men, checkout clerks, door-to-door solicitors, and (much to their chagrin) the Jehovah's Witnesses and Mormons who made their missionary rounds. She was a fixture in town: leaning on shop counters, holding doors ajar, blocking grocery aisles, her head canted to the side, frizzled red hair escaping straw hats and knit caps, waiting for the inevitable recognition and blush to cross some poor mark's face. She was a favorite at the post office, where – if the talk at Salty's could be trusted – the new male-identifying postal carriers were initiated by her during the holiday season, when she insisted on some complicated system of insurance, registration and certification of all her shipping to nieces and nephews (priority or not), just to see if they could keep a straight face through her various renditions of "package." Apparently, no one had ever known her to repeat the same material. Many of the younger men, despite growing up digitally native, had to go online to look up her references, and could not believe this sweet old woman could be referencing acts so uncommonly filthy. Deborah may have been Tracy's mother's age and worn a similar shade of lipstick, but the similarities ended there.

Once Tracy asked Deb why she never pursued any given man beyond the verbal attack. "Why should I let myself get tied down?" Deb had answered. "There's too much field to play." By "field" Tracy suspected Deb meant the endless supply of made-to-order supplies she had trucked right to her front door, especially in summer, when the men (and they were still mostly men) wore their summer uniform shorts. The internet had only expanded Deb's options. Tracy wouldn't be surprised if local companies included special information about Deborah Landry in their training materials. She had first been introduced to Deb through the tree-trimming business, Shade LLC, when Greg came home from a bid talking about a "crazy old lady" who asked about "oak wilt" among the work crew and offered to "give them a hand." When he returned to fell a tree overhanging her garage, she called him a stallion, asked if she could brush his hair, and then smacked him on the ass with a hairbrush as he came down the ladder.

Deborah's other habit that only a few people knew of, was that she was never sober after six o'clock – she opened a bottle at 5:30 sharp. Tracy checked on her most nights, crossing their back yards if the lights were left on too long. Every wine glass in the house was smeared with that same shade of lipstick that never seemed to wash off, and the danger of summer was that the long evening hours sometime tricked Deb into thinking she could begin a second bottle in the dusky light.

The first day on the road from Idaho, Tracy had driven about ten hours. She was almost to the Montana line before she stopped. The dogs rode well. Smoke was her co-pilot, sitting in the passenger seat, watching out the window, curling up and sleeping when she got tired. Red slept curled tight at the front of the mattress, just behind the center console, and Stella stretched out sideways, snoring most of the time in the back. At the first stop, Tracy realized she didn't have any leashes, the dogs didn't have any collars, and she didn't know how they'd react to this busy wayside with cars and semis alongside I-90. Luckily there was a field adjacent to the back of the lot, and the dogs stuck close and came when she called. She ignored the dirty looks from passing motorists who eyed the woman with the three dangerous-looking dogs running loose. They held their miniature poodles and yorkies close to their chests. She pulled off at the next exit, found a Walmart and bought collars and leashes, various treats, a few chew toys.

They slept in truck stop parking lots the two nights they were on the road. Smoke would curl up in the passenger seat. Red made herself small, and Stella would stretch out next to Tracy, same as in the bed in Aaron's cabin. If they heard a noise in the night, she'd hear Stella raise her head, alert. The pits would bark if someone approached the van, or if they needed a pit stop of their own, or when they slowed to pull into a gas station or drive through for food. She never heard Stella bark.

Somewhere in Montana she called Deb to thank her for picking up the mail, let her know she was on her way, and that she'd be home in a few days. She left a message on her machine.

Somewhere crossing the Dakotas, she called Cal. She'd been ignoring the recent call alerts since she'd left Aaron's cabin to run errands in Moscow that first week. Unfortunately, he answered. She told him she'd been out of town, a family emergency. No, she didn't really want to talk about it over the phone. She'd call him when she got back home. She was driving from Idaho with three dogs in a panel van. She heard him laugh, could imagine his mouth and his beard when he laughed. "That must be some story," he said.

"Yeah," she said.

"I'm allergic to dogs," he said.

"Oh." She paused, looked across the lot to where the van was parked. The dogs were lying down on their leashes in the shade of one of the rest stop trees. "I'll call you in a few days."

Tracy hadn't been out on an actual date in two years, not since she and Greg dissolved their seven-year relationship and five-year business partnership. For the tree-trimming business, they'd owned a dump trunk, a bucket truck, two pickups, and had had a crew of four part-time guys. Moving out of the house they'd shared had been the easy part. Moving on from Shade LLC had been harder.

For five years, in between joining the work crew to run a chainsaw and carry brush and scrub, Tracy scheduled appointments, kept track of invoices and payments, paid quarterly taxes, ran background checks on job applicants (which included an inordinate number of registered sex offenders and ex-cons), and sent out bids and bill reminders. Shade LLC was known for being fair with their bids, mostly on-time with their work, and understanding of late payments and IOUs. Tracy was the muscle, as it were, behind

Greg's sweet, hippie façade. He'd lope to the work site, long hair pulled back into a ponytail, and most home owners mistook him for one of his own crew. But Tracy's no-nonsense demeanor reassured them. When scheduling jobs and bids, her professionalism came through on paper and the necessary voice mail and email correspondences. She made sure the ragtag work crew tidied up after themselves, worked clean, and didn't stare at any teenage daughters.

So when Tracy did the quarterly close look at the books and the scheduling (a regular task she set herself, especially given the pasts of some of guys they hired on the work crew), she hadn't been all that surprised to find some missing hours between when the crew's logged hours ended and when the trucks and equipment were checked in. What had surprised her was that the missing hours and equipment were Greg's. The gas logs, too, showed more use than would have been explained by regular errands and stopping in town for any number of last-minute purchases. No, this was a different kind of impulse. A few casual questions revealed some extra work at that lake cottage around the far end, nearly at the other end of the county. Most of the crew seemed wholly innocent, but Luke (who'd worked for them for nearly two years) couldn't meet her eyes.

When she and Greg had first started dating, and then moved in together after just a few months, and then started building the house on the land Tracy had bought, he'd been continually surprised by her appetite for sex. Later, after they'd settled down a bit, he'd confided that he wasn't sure he'd be able to keep up. They'd be lazing around on a weekend, watching TV, and she'd take him into her mouth, for a quickie on the couch. They never just had sex once; it was usually multiples. Once they started the business, they made their own hours, so there was time in the evening, in the morning, time for a nooner at lunch. Tracy was adventurous, asking Greg to try things he hadn't before. On more than one occasion, when she whispered something into his ear, he had to stop and ask for clarification before he tried whatever it was she suggested. And when Tracy was about to come, she'd be very clear: "Lay still, legs together," she'd say, and he'd do what she said until she finished, always on top. Tracy would collapse on top of Greg, her body fitting exactly on top of his, toes to toes, shoulders touching, in the hay bale house in the woods on the land they'd cleared together.

But those last few years, when she'd feel Greg's body wake in the morning, and he'd roll over toward her, pressing his body along the length of her, his cock stiffening, she'd resent it, resent him; his needs, his body that woke every morning expecting the same thing. Things were different, but she wasn't sure why. She'd come to think of her morning alarm as 'the penis metronome,' tapping against her hip, waking her. She'd try to slowly draw away from him, slink out of the bed, quietly make coffee. When he'd walk out to the kitchen, long hair askew, asking the beginning of some question "Baby?," she'd be sure to be busy doing something on the computer, or returning calls for bids, so it wouldn't look like she'd chosen to leave their bed for any reason other than work.

When it became clear Greg had begun his own work at that job site, even after all the trees were trimmed and groomed and not a bit of gypsy moth infestation could be found, Tracy walked out of their house, past the idling trucks. The work crew had just shed their shirts and cracked open a few beers – they nodded at their boss as she walked to her car, a used Subaru, got in, started it up, and backed out of the drive without even checking the rearview mirror. Whether they knew or not what the second-in-command was doing all those afternoons he said he had to "check" on an "off-the-books job site" wasn't clear. But they all knew Tracy didn't do anything off the books.

What she couldn't stop thinking about was how Greg could put his dick into that woman and then come home and put his dick into her.

She spent two years licking her wounds.

To be fair, sometimes she had help. While she hadn't 'dated,' she hadn't been lonely, either. There were the occasional hookups. Not wanting to risk entanglements, she would ensure that they were truly passing through or visiting short-term at a summer rental. There were the opportunities that presented themselves to her when she was out of town. There was her one local standby, an older man, a sometimes business acquaintance of her father, who she'd briefly dallied with the summer between her sophomore and junior year of college. He was always available for some comfort and never interested in more than that. Comfort was comfort and boredom was boredom. Bodies, after all, were only bodies – pleasure could be freely given and freely taken.

While Tracy was embarrassed with the way things had ended with Greg, she wasn't all that upset that they had ended. Their last few years together, he'd begun dropping hints, mentioning kids from time to time, thinking about whether and if a certain room could be turned into a nursery, re-telling a story one too many times about his grandparents with emphasis on family, on things passed down. It wasn't that Tracy didn't like kids, but she didn't feel any pull to have any of her own. If someone had asked if she was happy, or if she loved Greg, she would have answered "Yes," but mostly because she knew that's what she was supposed to say. She thought she had been in love once: he was a friend of her college roommate's, and she'd met him during junior year. Immediately it had been electric. Sitting next to him, his leg grazing hers, had jolted her. They both sat very still, silently pressing the outer edges of their thighs together under the tabletop, grinning dumbly, as they listened to their mutual friend talk, sipping their coffees. They'd made plans to see each other the following weekend, and the weekend after that. By midweek, Tracy would be overcome with anxiety. Each thing she did would be imbued with some kind of importance – the last trip to the gas station before she saw him, sitting on a high stool waiting until the last minute to walk to the door she'd exit before getting into the car to drive to meet him. She couldn't be sure, but she'd swear she was having heart palpitations. They'd only spent one night in bed, and hadn't even had sex (he'd wanted to wait), but had lain fully-clothed, stretched length-wise, breathing the same air, touching faces and hands and arms. He started every sentence with her name and a little exhale, "Ah, Tracy..." as if everything was an endearment. It was awful: she couldn't breathe, she couldn't sleep, couldn't relax or concentrate or read or do anything but think about him. After three weeks, she called to tell him she didn't want to see him again.

After that close call with love, she'd stuck to hookups and guys who wouldn't ask very much of her. She remembered one townie, a sweet guy really, who she killed time with for a few months after her close call. She didn't know if he was good in bed, or if they just fit, but almost as soon as she climbed on top, she'd be half-way there and in minutes, good and gone. Sometimes, she'd give him a sloppy kiss and roll off, falling asleep whether he was done or not. She remembered telling some friends this, bragging a little, thinking they'd laugh along, but they'd looked stricken. Tracy didn't get it – these were the same women who complained that their boyfriends did the same thing; she thought they'd appreciate her evening it out for all of womankind.

After leaving Greg and the business, Tracy took a job at the local elementary school, working in the office. It gave her the summers off, from mid-June to mid-August; then the teachers returned and the fall schedules needed to be organized. She liked assigning duties, getting people to agree, and checking off completed tasks. Whether budgets or people, she had a knack for making projects run smoothly. The casual office environment agreed with her, too. Most days she could wear jeans and sneakers, a clean t-shirt and cardigan and look presentable, her shoulder-length hair pulled into a loose ponytail, her only adornment the real diamond studs in her earlobes. She liked calling and offering the people on the substitute roster a day's work; the regular rhythm of payroll, and preparing curriculum and lesson-plan binders for new teachers. She even liked contacting parents to deal with discipline issues and complaints about their 'little darlings.' Everyone's child was a 'little darling.' After work, she'd sometimes have a beer with the teachers. She had her summers for projects, to garden or do a work-share at the local organic farm. Money wasn't an issue.

One thing Tracy had needed was a new place to live. Her home with Greg they'd built together, but it had been mostly his hands involved in everything. She'd been happy to walk away from that. And since the house's use of green construction techniques seemed new to people around here – a little circumspect – there was no way the market assessment would have adequately valued the little house and its myriad, thoughtful design choices. After a few too many conversations about R-value and passive solar heat, watching the assessor's eyes glaze over, she arranged to gift the house and the small parcel of land it sat on to Greg. It was the business's value she really cared about – that was the thing she'd built.

When she was still with Greg, gassing up the work trucks in town, she'd watched as the brick house across the street from the filling station fell into disrepair, unloved. It wasn't officially for sale, but she'd found a way to buy it, and set to work making the house something of her own. She hired out the major work: shoring up the foundation, replacing the missing and damaged brick, having re-pointing work done all over the house. While the drywallers worked inside, she cleared the yard – work that reminded her of

Shade LLC. She found broken children's toys and a pet cemetery in back, and under a layer of weeds, a forgotten brick patio. Filling the house with repaired and repainted finds from estate sales and junk stores brought her unreasonable pleasure. Sometimes, when she was searching through piles of disorder in a barn sale, or attacking an overgrown corner of the side yard, she'd be overcome with anticipation. It was as if some great discovery was waiting around the next corner, at the bottom of the next rust pile, or just beneath the tangled thistle and bindweed she was pulling. She would start breathing hard and could feel her heart beating, feel it in her ears. There was nothing to warrant this bodily response, but it came like clockwork, this search for the find – anticipation with no release. She never felt disappointed, just that she wanted to keep looking, keep working.

But Cal might complicate things – he seemed to think that she was gun-shy in ways that she wasn't. Cal had been asking her out for a few months ago and she finally said yes. He knew she was single. He'd started slow, smiling, then asking her how she was doing, maybe buying a beer if they both ended up at Salty's at the same time. That process began fall of last year. He had a beard that she liked – close cropped and dark brown, almost black. Little bits of silver showed here and there and she suspected he might be concerned about it. At times the grey seemed less than the time before, as if he'd gotten rid of it somehow. After those months of casual hellos, a few beers, he asked her out and she said no the first few times. Then he asked her to go bowling and she did; then as June began, to watch his nephew play one of the first games of the summer league. There were fireworks afterward and they'd each had a lukewarm beer and a terrible hot dog, with relish and mustard.

Summer games were played at the town park, adjacent to the high school grounds, only a half a mile from Tracy's house, but they'd ridden there in Cal's work truck, the tools jangling loose in the back, the windows rolled down. The temperature during the day had been in the mid-70's, but it still cooled at night. The elementary kids had finished that week, and by Friday the middle and high schools would be quiet too; just teachers and administrators finishing the semester's work, filing paperwork, entering reports and data into computers, and dealing with projects set aside until they couldn't be set aside anymore. Tracy had about one more week of easy work until her summer truly began and she was already itching for it. The amaryllis greens that signaled spring had showed early through the snow and had begun to die back, and the fern forest that ringed the north side of the house had started, the thick beginnings of ferns that looked like fists working their way out of the soil. By the time she left her last day of work next week, they would have unfurled and be too tough to simmer with butter and garlic. The summer started the way most summers did: the anticipation of fiddleheads and the cool evening temperatures teasing shoulders and arms and any other skin caught uncovered. Tracy didn't know what to make of Cal, or the music of his tools in the back of his truck.

After Cal walked her back to her porch, he'd kissed her and she'd thought maybe she tasted some of that mustard stuck in his beard. She'd kissed him back hard then, grinding her face against his beard, liking the rawness on her cheeks, imaging them reddened from the friction. She'd slowly pushed him backwards, until the back of his knees met the old wicker furniture she'd spray-painted Rustoleum neon green. But when she'd started to unbutton his jeans, he'd taken her hands in his. Even in this gesture, she could feel his sweetness, the way he was trying to slow her down. Her face was red and raw from his beard; she'd wanted to, but he said he'd call her the next day.

That next day he sent her a few sexy texts – not overt, but still. He probably thought he was daring, sending those texts; that she was a nice girl and he was wooing her or something, like she'd never gotten one before. Greg hadn't really been that kind of guy either. One time when a late spring snowstorm surprised them both, he'd sent: LOTTA FUCKIN SNOW and she'd teased him that it was almost a sext.

When the phone finally buzzed, she'd answered in her best fuck-me voice. But it had been her father, calling with the news that Aaron was dead.

Lucy

After an afternoon of errands and watching the jumbo loads fluff and dry on her Wednesday off, Lucy was loading the baskets of comforters into the hatchback at the laundromat. She saw the woman again walking the three dogs along the railroad trestle on Townline, behind the laundromat parking lot and the empty building that used to be the IGA, before the Walmart superstore with the grocery moved in across town. The two pits were walking her really, straining at the ends of their leashes, with the mastiff walking close to her side. Each time she'd seen the woman, it had been like this: the two dogs pulling her, the woman's body canted back, trying to counterbalance, and the big dog, her close-kept shadow, trucking right by her side.

Once she'd seen her in the twilight around the deserted baseball fields by the high school; once by the industrial park, where it had grown quiet since the muffler plant closed down and no new business took its place, and now here. The woman and her dogs backgrounded by the places in town that had been deserted and unpeopled. Lucy thought for a minute about Carla waiting at home, closed the hatchback, and crossed the parking lot, waving.

"Hello!" she yelled.

The woman stopped and the pits turned toward Lucy, barking happily and wagging their tails. She could see the woman tense up and put her hand on the mastiff.

"Hi," the woman said, warily.

Lucy stopped about ten feet away. She said loudly, "Beautiful dogs!"

"Thanks," the woman said and smiled. She pushed her bangs off of her forehead.

"Do you mind if I come a little closer? These two look friendly," Lucy said, pointing at the grey and red dogs, still wagging happily in her direction.

"Those two love people," the woman answered, as she looked down at the mastiff, who had now shifted position so that she was standing slightly in front of her person, head lowered, looking at Lucy. "This one…"

"Don't worry, I won't come any closer to you or your Bordeaux," she said. "I can tell she's not comfortable."

"OK," the woman answered. Lucy walked toward the pits and held out her hands, and once they'd given her the sniff over, she pet them lightly, but when they started to jump, she took a step back, said firmly "No," and waited for them to calm down with all eight paws on the ground before she'd pet them again. After a few tries at exuberance, the pits learned their lesson and waited happily for Lucy to pet them.

"That's a neat trick," the woman said, "getting them to stop jumping. I'll have to try that."

"I'm Lucy," Lucy said.

"Tracy."

"Nice to meet you. You've got beautiful dogs." And they were. Most people were too concentrated on the reputation of pit bulls to really look at dogs like these. The grey one was the same ethereal coloring people loved on Weimaraners. The red pit was tiny, probably no more than twenty-five pounds.

Tracy appreciated how Lucy talked directly to her, not staring at Stella or even acknowledging her. She had her hand resting on Stella's shoulders, and she could feel the muscles relax there after a moment. Lucy kept talking to the other dogs, kept up her soft-voiced patter, pretending there wasn't a hulking, drooling canine giving her the wary eye.

Tracy looked back up the railroad trestle and down Townline, checking for cars and other walkers. The big parking lot alongside the laundromat and the old grocery store was empty except for Lucy's hatchback. Tracy had taken to walking the dogs this route because they so rarely met other people, or their dogs, who presented different kinds of problems for different reasons. Stella liked other dogs but was wary of people; Smoke and Red loved people but not dogs. Walking all three of the dogs was almost more than Tracy could handle. With no one around, and Lucy being so friendly, she dropped the pits' leashes. Lucy picked them right up.

"What did you call this one – a Bordo?" Tracy asked.

"Bordeaux. She's a French mastiff, isn't she?"'

"I don't know what she is..." Tracy admitted, smiling sheepishly at Lucy. "I don't really know much about dogs at all."

"How does a woman who doesn't know much about dogs end up with these dogs?" Lucy asked.

"Good question. I inherited them. You've got Red and Smoke there. And this is Stella." As Tracy said her name, Stella looked up at her and leaned into her body, nearly knocking her over.

"Apt names," Lucy looked down at the pits, "and I'm sorry for your loss." Lucy could see Tracy swallow, but she didn't say anything. "And I bet Stella is your best friend, but only loves you."

"That's about right," Tracy sighed, then took a deep breath and let her shoulders fall. Since she'd come back from Idaho, and news of Aaron's death had spread, Tracy had heard this phrase a hundred times, *I'm sorry for your loss,* from nearly everyone she saw. For years, she'd thought she was living an anonymous life in her own town, that she was just 'Tracy,' not "Tracy Luft." But apparently everyone did know who she was, who her parents were, and that her brother had killed himself. The first few times a stranger offered condolences, out of the blue, when bagging her groceries, or handing back her change at the gas station across the street from her house, she'd teared up. By now she was used to it, and the open wound of Aaron's death had begun to close, maybe scab a little. When Lucy said it, she looked right into Tracy's eyes, holding them in a way that was both comforting and aggressive.

Lucy sat down on the cement curb that ringed the back of the asphalt parking lot, facing away from Tracy and Stella. Smoke and Red came around in front of her, kissing her face while Lucy spoke low to them, getting them to lie down. She reached into the pocket of her fleece vest, and threw a couple of dog treats behind her.

"While I'm facing this way, why don't you come a little closer?" she said out of the corner of her mouth to Tracy, without turning her head. Stella had already picked up the scent of whatever it was that had been thrown in her direction, and was diligently sniffing in Lucy's direction, moving toward the strange woman.

"You know dogs." Tracy said.

"Yup," Lucy answered, throwing more treats behind her, as Stella made her slow way into the safe space occasioned by the strange woman's lack of interest in her. They stayed there, Tracy and Lucy, talking for another twenty minutes. Lucy told her she worked at the vet clinic on Prospect Street, and told Tracy to bring the dogs in. She said she didn't mean to be pushy, but the dogs needed to be licensed in town, especially being the kind of dogs that attract attention, and that they'd need a vet exam and to be certified and up-to-date on vaccinations. Lucy also offered obedience lessons, temperament testing, and in-home work through her company *Pawsitive Solutions* (she produced a card from her pocket). She offered to help Tracy with leash training for Smoke and Red (which they sorely needed), positive conditioning for Stella and maybe some dog talk with Tracy. She'd given the dogs the entire contents of her pockets, homemade liver treats, and offered to share the recipe with Tracy. She also spelled out *Dogue de Bordeaux* for Tracy, so she could look it up and do some research.

By the end of their meeting, Smoke was laying on her back between Lucy's legs, belly-up for the new friend's hands, looking like a carp, silver-scaled and spawning in the weeds. Red's entire body had been lightly gone over, and when Lucy's fingers found a particularly dense whorl of scars, she'd whispered, "Oh baby girl..." into the freckled ear while the little dog's tail thumped in the scrub nettle and chicory striving through the cracked asphalt lot. Even Stella had laid down behind Lucy (in her shadow but not touching her, panting, after burying her jowls in the woman's curly hair for several big inhales and exhales). Lucy didn't even seem to mind the Stella-evidence that adorned the back of her shirt: dried slicks of drool that caught the late sunlight.

On the drive out of town to the farm, Lucy could see the clouds building up, a storm coming, one of those late June events that drenched them up on the hill and washed away any dirt not yet claimed by spreading green. She knew Carla would be watching the clouds too, worrying that Lucy wasn't home, anxious for the chores in the barn, the animals that needed tending. When she pulled in the garage and grabbed the baskets from the back, Carla was already holding open the door at the top of the ramp, giving her the eye.

"I know, I know, but I met the woman with the dogs. We..."

"Animals first. We'll talk at dinner." Carla said, handing her the milk bottle.

Lucy headed out to the barn to bottle-feed the tiny goat first, their newest orphan. They'd gotten a call a few weeks ago about a goat whose mother had died and whether they could take the baby. Since then, they'd been bottle-feeding the little guy, and he lived in a smaller enclosure (hastily put together of fence materials) inside the open area of the big barn. When he saw Lucy coming with the bottle, he started jumping all over the inside of his pen, stirring up his pen-mates, the older kid, and the shy adult goat, whom they'd rescued from a fence where she'd been caught with her neck tangled in the wire for who knows how long. Lucy sat on the overturned bucket and the baby jumped into her lap, and started sucking hard on the bottle.

The other animals gathered outside the pen, knowing their turns were coming. There were two alpaca-llama mixes that nobody wanted because the wool was neither alpaca nor llama. There were three horses with various problems, a skittish watch donkey, ducks and geese, and guinea fowl. Lucy watered and fed all the animals before the storm hit. If she'd had time, she would have spent more of it with the kittens. They'd recently got two little kittens to train as barn cats. Each day they tried to play with them with the toy mice, then reward them with some cat food, triggering the play and food impulse, so they'd learn to hunt the mice that infested the barn.

Ever since Lucy was little, she'd been bringing home the hurt, lost, and abandoned. Her parents were mostly good about it, knowing it was at least partially their fault. When she was really little, maybe six or so, their golden retriever, Lou, had found two kittens one winter and brought them home, hid them in his bed in the garage, and tried to keep them alive. Lucy found them all one morning. Lou was curled up very tightly around his found-lings, but when Lucy finally lured him up with a strip of fresh bacon, the kittens were frozen solid.

And there was her friend in high school, Kim, whose parents belonged to some insular religious sect. When they found out Kim had a boyfriend, they threw her out of the house, tossing all her clothes and belongings out the windows of her second story bedroom. She'd called Lucy and they'd both gathered the things scattered around the wide lawn, while Kim's family watched from the windows, behind the doors they'd locked, while their daughter and her heathen friend alternately cried and swore at them.

Lucy remembered how Kim had still been in her pajamas, a long old-lady nightgown with many, many buttons down the front, and thick rag socks that became sopping with the morning dew. She'd picked Kim's shirts and skirts off the shrubs that grew all around the house, holding big armfuls of clothing and carrying them to the car. When she picked several pairs of Kim's underwear off a pink-blooming spirea right in front of the living room bay window, she'd looked up to see Kim's father, looking down on her through the glass, with such a look of hatred on his face, she'd felt slapped.

Kim stayed with them for three nights and rode to school and back with Lucy. One night she'd heard her father on the phone with Kim's father, and her father sounded tired, but his voice was pitched low, and he spoke very slowly.

"I suggest you do call the police. I already have. You threw your fifteen-year old daughter out of her house." Lucy didn't know if her father had called the police or not, but later that night a car pulled into their driveway and sat there for hours with the headlights on, trained on their front door. Her father locked the doors – they never locked the doors – and they all sat in the living room, watching TV; her mother and father, Lucy, Kim, her brothers, the telephone right beside them on the end table. Kim went home after that and Lucy never saw her again. When she was packing her things, she told Lucy it was what she wanted.

Lucy knew that most people thought Carla was another of her 'rescues.' Carla was older, sixty-two to Lucy's forty-five. And Carla's health and mobility issues affected their lives in some ways. She wasn't able to care for the animals in the barn the way Lucy was, but she handled the birds, cats, and dogs who lived in the house. She used canes to get around in the house and when they went out, and they'd already installed ramps to help with walking and for when Carla needed a chair. Their next big investment was the indoor swimming pool they'd be putting in next year – the doctors had said this kind of exercise, no impact, was the best thing for Carla. From the outside, if people looked at lean and athletic Lucy, working full-time at the vet clinic plus her own business on the side and then older, thicker, and (if Lucy was honest) stereotypical lesbian-looking Carla, with her buzzcut grey hair, jeans and flannels, they'd think that Lucy was settling. But if it wasn't for Carla, Lucy probably wouldn't even be alive.

After meeting Tracy and the dogs, and the hurry-up chores in the barn, Lucy and Carla sat down to dinner together with the inside animals at their feet – some seeking comfort from the storm, its barometric spikes and sudden sounds, some just needing acknowledgement and then finding their own safe spaces on the tops of couches or under beds. It was the first big summer storm. Thunder shook the house and lightning flashes cast everything into black and white relief. In the barn, it would have been deafening, pelting the metal roof. Out the windows, the fat drops splattered the dirt and shit in the yard (where the geese and guinea fowl congregated into some sort of reverse conflagration) until the dust was tamped down to a mat of brown mud and the geese's pond had overlapped its rock border and filled the front lawn.

The storm continued through the night. The dogs were crated, like they were every night. Gusts of wind whipped the curtains in the bedroom. The storm turned Lucy on – storms always had. Carla was thankful for this, the way this distracted her, had almost conditioned her out of her fear when they were first together. Lucy had once told her that she could tell when a storm was coming; that her skin began to spark, like some science class static electricity experiment, begging for touch. Her excitement almost made Carla forget what it was like to grow up in a place with no basement, no interior room without windows, listening carefully for the sirens, the rumble that was said to sound like a freight train when it was coming (although knowing there was nowhere safe to go anyway made the careful listening a kind of purgatorial ritual). Mornings they'd hear some nearby town had been wiped out. Carla's mother would joke that God must hate trailer parks; her father's grunt Carla always took as assent. Even after she got away from the trailer and was living in a house on a foundation, with a basement, with doors that weren't hollow-core, the fear followed her. It followed her until she and Lucy finally left Iowa.

Lucy had known she liked girls long before Kim. She'd always known. In grade school and high school, she'd had intense friendships with girls and by eleven she'd had her first official make-out session, with her best friend Michelle that had ended inexplicably with them rolling around in the ditch in back of Michelle's house. Lucy still associated desire with the smell of newly-cut grass and girl-sweat, the tang of strawberry shampoo. Although Michelle had been embarrassed and they'd never rolled around in the ditch again, for Lucy that afternoon had been revelatory. She'd kept that memory inside her all through high school, until she would go away to college, where there was something called a GLA and a Big Dyke Party. On National Coming Out Day, she called her parents.

Her father answered. "Hi Dad," and Lucy's voice was singing, excited, maybe a little anxious. In the GLA meetings, they'd talked about the various ways these conversations could go. But Lucy was confident, thinking of her father sticking up for Kim, thinking of her mother telling her *you can always talk to us*, asking *do you have any questions?* as she'd hang red and green condoms on the Christmas tree, much to the chagrin of her and her brothers, their faces red in flickering twinkle-lights.

"I'm calling because it's National Coming Out Day," Lucy said, breathlessly.

"What?" her father said, and she could hear the television getting quieter in the background as he either walked into the other room or turned down the volume.

"It's National Coming Out Day," Lucy continued, "and I'm calling to tell you I'm a lesbian."

"Oh."

"Dad?"

"I'm here," he said and then there was quiet. Lucy breathed and her father breathed at the other end of the line. "Why did you tell me?"

If that was odd, a little anticlimactic, it didn't seem to change anything. He passed the phone to Lucy's mother, where she repeated her pronouncement. Lucy's mother said she knew, that she'd always known, then asked how school was going and if she had any plans for summer.

The following year, Lucy and her then-girlfriend Elsa, packed up the car in Ann Arbor and drove home for spring break. She'd given her parents a heads-up and they'd set up the guest room for Elsa. Her mother explained that if she'd been bringing a boyfriend home, he'd be sleeping in the guest room, and they weren't going to treat Elsa any differently, which was kind of sweet. But that night, her father had offered Elsa a cigar, poured her a glass of scotch. Lucy's father didn't smoke cigars, and Elsa looked at her, bewildered, unsure what to make of this strange offer. Lucy and her mother looked similarly bewildered. But Elsa was a good sport, puffing the spicy sweet stogie, sending rings of smoke to the ceiling, while Lucy and her mother watched, half-smiling. The next morning, the taste of misunderstanding had settled into her mouth and she shared it with Lucy in several long, stolen kisses. For the next six months, while she and Elsa were still together, it became a favorite story of theirs to tell: how Lucy's awkward father had tried to welcome her girlfriend, assumed that Lucy must be the femme in the relationship. That too, was kind of sweet.

When it ended with Elsa, it was amicable. Graduation was nearing and Elsa was planning to road trip to California. She had this idea that with her Saturn, she could stop at dealerships and take advantage of free donuts and coffee to cut down on food costs. She'd be traveling with Kirby, her big-boned mutt, and would sleep wherever, stopping along the way to do odd jobs for cash. Kirby would be protection for a woman traveling alone, although Elsa didn't look like a woman to mess with anyway. She was six feet two, big-boned herself, with long red hair that made her look like a Viking warrior. She'd been known to wear a chain mail bra just for fun. On her right bicep, she'd had Kirby's name tattooed.

When Lucy graduated, she didn't know what she was going to do. She'd been an environmental science major, done an internship with a local land conservation group, but thought that maybe there'd be options in northern California, which just so happened to be where Elsa ended up. If Elsa could travel across country on her own, like a woman warrior, then Lucy could too. She got as far as Waterloo, Iowa before her car blew a head gasket.

She'd planned to only stay there as long as it took to make the money to pay for car repairs, but she'd underestimated the seriousness of a blown head gasket. The car was basically useless. The week-to-week hotel she'd found cost more than she'd planned. She ended up waitressing at a diner, close enough that she could walk to and from work. After a few weeks, one of the older waitresses had taken a liking to her, sometimes bringing her leftovers in opaque Tupperware with stiff pastel lids that she reassured Lucy she didn't have to return, although she always washed them carefully in the hotel bathroom and brought them back. When the part-time cook caught her behind the dumpster after everyone else had left, she finally realized why her parents had worried about her, why the older waitress had kept asking *you all alone honey?*, why everyone seemed startled by the idea of a young woman traveling across the country alone. The world was full of danger and unimaginable pain. It kept coming and coming. Even when she said its name, the name she'd said for weeks, the face she'd known through multiple shifts, the eyes that had seemed friendly and open, the hand that had sometimes brushed hers when handing over a plate of runny egg yolks and grizzled hash browns, it wouldn't answer. It made her a thing – a ragdoll, a sack of garbage, a cigarette butt. Not a person.

Every morning afterward it seemed someone was knocking on the motel room door. She'd burrow deeper into the pillows and stale sheets. Sometimes she'd hear the voice of housekeeping, or the hotel management, and once the waitress from the diner. She'd moan, and cover her head with more pillows. She didn't answer. Finally, the insistent knocking was followed by the sound of a key in the door, but she'd secured the chain.

"Miss," the woman's voice said. "Miss?"

"Uh huh," Lucy half-grunted.

"Miss," the woman's voice continued, officious. "I've got some mail for you and your bill." There was a sound of papers being slid under the door.

"OK," Lucy was fully awake this time and she sat up.

"Miss, you were paid up through the week, but that week ended yesterday."

"Oh, I'll take another week," Lucy said. "Let me get my card..."

"Miss, we tried to charge the card yesterday, but it was denied. And also Miss..." the voice paused, "there's someone here to see you." In the background came another voice.

"Lucy honey, can I talk to you?" It was Peggy from the diner. Lucy groaned.

"Lucy, I've paid your bill for you, so you owe me a talk." Peggy's voice was stern, the voice she used with truckers who got fresh at the diner, or the teenaged dishwashers who couldn't be bothered to scrub the pots before leaving at the end of their shift.

"Coming," Lucy said, knowing that to argue with Peggy was useless.

When she let Peggy in, and Peggy looked around the room at the closed curtains, the stiff and dirty sheets, Lucy stiff and dirty herself, with purpled bruises just starting to fade to watery green around her jaw and neck, she didn't say anything else, but took the girl in her arms and sat with her on the edge of the bed where Lucy shuddered her utterly quiet body-wracking sobs. When everything was still again, Peggy stood up and started putting Lucy's things into her duffel bags while Lucy stayed right where she was, not understanding.

"Come on, girl," Peggy said. "You're coming home with me."

Peggy lived on a horse farm, as it turned out. There were stables where people boarded their horses and came out to ride. The stables were set away from the house, and for the first two weeks, it was just Peggy and Lucy. She set Lucy up in the spare room and didn't ask too many questions. Peggy was taking extra shifts at the diner since they'd lost Lucy as a waitress and the part-time cook had taken off, too. The first time Peggy mentioned this, Lucy had startled, and Peggy looked at her and said "Uh huh," and didn't mention it again. She showed Lucy how to lock the doors after she left, left her a list of phone numbers to reach Peggy, the neighbors, and her sister Carla, who was traveling but would be back soon. She introduced Lucy to the traveling vet Dr. Shattuck, the stable workers, Seth and Henry, but told her they stayed out in the stables and wouldn't bother her.

After those two weeks, Carla came back and Lucy warmed to her, to her presence. She was friendly, but quiet, and gave Lucy the space she needed, but also seemed to know when Lucy needed and could handle a little pressure. Looking back at that time later, Lucy would come to see it as her rehabilitation. One day Carla mentioned at breakfast that she could use a little help with a new foal that was born during the night. The next day, she mentioned that Lucy could help her with paperwork while she checked in a new horse. Then it was helping Carla with Seth's chores when he was on vacation. Slowly, Carla brought Lucy into the horses' orbits and let the horses do the work; let these huge sleek animals, their long flanks and big eyes, wide nostrils, and smooth muscles, start their impromptu equine therapy. The immensity of touch. When they were in the barn working together, Lucy would watch Carla's way with the horses and see the same kinds of interactions that Carla had with her: the low steady talk, the light touch, the offer of something sweet to convince the animal to come to her. Carla was *gentling* her.

Lucy stayed with Peggy and Carla for two years. As she and Carla fell in love, Peggy pretended not to notice, but Lucy knew she was happy for them both. When their great aunt died, leaving Peggy and Carla a lump sum because she'd had no children of her own, they toasted the woman with a big bottle of champagne and cursed their parents, both long dead.

"Well, little sister," Peggy said, slurring ever so slightly, "what now?"

"Let's get the fuck out of here," Carla answered, toasting her sister, then Lucy. Her happiness was sloppy, contagious. Peggy laughed her big open-mouthed laugh and tossed back her glass. Peggy and Carla had grown up poor, scrunched into a double-wide with their parents, and moved and moved again, finally moving into this house, taking on the horse farm and all its headaches, working part-time job after part-time job, for as long as they could both remember.

"What do you think Luce?" Peggy asked.

"Well, it's not my decision to make," Lucy answered. She was so thankful to these women, these sisters, who had saved her: first Peggy from that hotel room where she was wasting away, too afraid to even call her parents, and then Carla, from all the fears that followed her here; and then Carla again, in ways she couldn't even count and name. When she talked to her parents now, she was so proud of the life she had with Carla and her sister, with the horses, the daily life she had getting up and caring for these animals, caring for each other.

"I say we get married," Carla said.

"Carla!" Peggy hooted, grinning again her wide-open smile.

"Wouldn't that be something," Lucy said. Was that something she could even imagine? Earlier that August, President Clinton had signed an executive order and for the first time the phrase "sexual orientation" was included. It had something to do with security clearance, but that didn't have anything to do with Lucy's life. Still, including that phrase must mean something. Maybe the something it meant was that someday, if Carla asked her to marry her, and she said *Yes* that it would mean they could marry.

"We could get engaged," Carla said. Peggy's head was bobbing up and down maniacally.

"Are you asking?"

"Lucy Stillwater, will you marry me?" Carla smiled, taking her hand, knocking over her glass of champagne in the process.

"Yes," Lucy said, the sticky bubbles soaking into her horse manure-stained jean shorts, while the sun sank low behind the barn, an impossible red.

By the time they finally left the horse farm that winter, it was a near blizzard. They caravanned east, two loaded-down cars and a U-Haul, with Carla driving. Peggy and Carla split the inheritance. Peggy moved to the Quad Cities into a little apartment, but it felt "downright cosmopolitan" to her; Carla and Lucy helped her move then headed north. They'd settled on a town in central Wisconsin, a place neither of them had ever been, but they'd bought a farmette. It was about two hours from Lucy's parents (a distance they'd decided was just about right). There was a barn, a pole building, a ranch house, and twenty acres. They hoped to do something with animals (Lucy planned to look into behavioral training); maybe boarding and training, maybe dogs or horses – who knows? The money from Carla's aunt made for a nice little nest egg and a twenty percent down payment. Lucy's dad helped them develop an investment portfolio that would grow and provide regular payouts without cutting into the principal.

Fences

Earlier in that last week of June, the same week Tracy happened to meet Lucy, Tracy had made the rounds of the neighbors, gently informing them of her intention to put a privacy fence around the backyard. The two side neighbors seemed relieved. Ever since she'd come back with the dogs, they'd been shooting worried glances in her direction when the dogs were on their tie-outs. Smoke and Red generally ended up in a tangled mess, yelping for Tracy's help within five minutes, while Stella found a shady spot and looked askance at the other two dogs. In general, the tie outs weren't working anyway, resulting in only a few minutes of peace before chaos descended. The older couple generally shot worried looks in her direction anyway, long before the dogs. They worried about her *living all by herself,* about *you young women and your ideas,* about *this dangerous world and how it'll catch up with you.* The other family with the two toddlers had been keeping their kids out of sight for the two weeks since she'd been home, loading them into side-by-side strollers and trucking to the neighborhood park, rather than playing on the backyard swing set. She'd hoped to make friends between the kids and Smoke and Red, but when the mother, Jen, saw that the "puppies" her little angels were squealing over were pit bulls, she'd closed the side windows, blinds, and privacy curtains and had done no more than curtly nod to Tracy when they'd meet at the front mailboxes.

Deb had seemed quite upset by the fence plan. Tracy reassured her that there'd be a gate in back, and that their regular visits wouldn't change at all, but the fence was symbolic as well as actual, a point Deb made clear by quoting Frost the following night, in a warbling voice lubricated by a bottle of Beaujolais. Tracy knew she was serious, but between the lipstick staining her front tooth, and the sun hat having fallen onto her back so that its chin cord appeared to be choking her, it was hard to keep a straight face. Deb forgave her though, when she saw the work crew who showed up. She dragged a lawn chair to the edge of her lot line, brought out a pitcher of lemonade and clapped when the men took their shirts off at about 10:30. When Tracy stopped mixing concrete to tell her to cool it, Deb waved her off and told her she was just enjoying the show.

Tracy had gone into the Tru-Valu to order materials and delivery and had been surprised to see Luke behind the counter, but remembered that she'd given him a glowing reference last winter. When they'd hired Luke for Shade LLC, he'd just gotten out of the local jail but, based on his convictions, should have been in prison. He must have known someone to be kept at the local jail, with its smaller population and good work program; kept close to his family and friends. And after working with Luke for a few weeks, she couldn't imagine what had happened anyway. When she'd done a records search on him, she found exactly what he'd self-reported: a large number of theft convictions, all pled down to misdemeanors. When she googled him, the reports seemed to suggest larger thefts, surely more than the $1,000 maximum of his plea agreements. Even stranger, for a character reference, he'd listed the owner of the company he'd been convicted of stealing from – his former boss. Her curiosity was piqued; she called the boss. He answered on the third ring.

"Yes, hello, I'm calling for a reference on Luke Skelfreg. This is Tracy Luft."

"Well, hello, Miss, I was expecting your call a few weeks ago. Luke said you run a tight operation over there," the man said.

Tracy stumbled, "Um, well, uh... you talked to Luke?"

"Sure," the man said. "He was over for dinner last night."

"Didn't he... uh, didn't he go to jail for stealing from you? Large equipment?"

"Yes, Miss, he did."

"And you had him over for dinner?"

The man laughed. "Can I speak frankly, Miss?"

"Sure."

"Luke fucked up. He knows he fucked up. He paid for it. He went to jail. He paid restitution. That conviction will be following him around the rest of his life and he'll be thinking about what he did for all that time," He paused. "But I trust Luke. I'd hire him again in a minute. I've offered, but he turned me down, said it wouldn't be right."

"Oh."

"I'd trust him with my business, with my home, with my kids. Hell – I'd trust him with my dog," he laughed. Tracy was silent.

"Your dog?" she asked.

"You don't have a dog, do you Miss?"

"No, I don't. Or kids." She answered.

"Oh, right. I probably shouldn't have worded it like that, not in that order. Don't tell my wife I said it quite that way," and he laughed again. "Look. Keep Luke on. He'll be your best employee."

Tracy had thought of that conversation when it was Luke who, inadvertently, had confirmed her suspicions about Greg. She'd thought of it again when Tru-Valu had called for a reference. She'd tried to do Luke justice over the phone, but didn't think there was any way to quite match the charm of the reference his old boss had given him – the boss he'd stolen from, who'd been a character witness for him at his sentencing, who'd continued to welcome Luke into his home, and help him in any way he could. She thought of that reference now, as she smiled at Luke across the counter of the hardware store, ordering materials for the fence. She'd trust him with her dogs, now that she knew what that meant.

She ordered fencing panels (pre-made, six-foot high, stockade style), Quikcrete, posts, gate hinges, some extra wood, and rented a post-hole digging machine. As she was going over her sketches, doing her own calculations with pencil and the calculator on her phone, Luke asked if she needed help. She smiled. "Sure – you got someone in mind?"

When he showed up that Saturday morning, seven sharp, she was a little taken aback by the crew. It was Luke, Cal, and a boy she didn't know. Luke introduced his cousin, Ian. Tracy smiled shyly at Cal, then turned to Luke. "OK, I know, I know, but he said he'd be happy to help as long as you paid him decent," and Luke threw his hands up. Cal smirked.

She'd seen Cal once since she'd gotten back from Idaho. She'd called that week and they'd met at Salty's for a beer. She told the abbreviated story of Aaron (he hadn't heard about it from her, but had known about her brother, his troubles). She told him she now had three dogs and they were a bit of a handful, and that she wasn't sure how much time she'd have for a relationship. As she said this, she could feel how it was both true and not true, how the dogs were a useful excuse. Stella could make things hard, but if he wanted to invest a little time – and Cal made clear it he was willing to invest time – even Stella wasn't really an impediment. Smoke and Red loved people. Cal had put his hand on her back when she talked about Aaron taking pills, and she'd stiffened, not unlike Stella did with new people. He'd felt it and gingerly removed his hand.

"And your allergies…" she'd said.

"I can take a Zyrtek," he'd said.

Most of the rest of the conversation had continued like that: Tracy bringing up things to push him away, Cal countering with ways they could still spend time together. By the end of the second beer, they were both tired. Tracy left first, saying she had to get home to see to the dogs, and Cal stayed for a third.

So when Tracy saw that Luke had included Cal in the work crew she wondered whose idea it was and how much Luke knew. When Luke saw the backyard, he realized how much he'd forgotten about Tracy. There were utility flags fluttering on their wire stakes, marking underground lines and pipes, duly placed before any digging. The lot lines had been clearly marked, and she'd run cord for where the fence would go, measuring and marking eight-foot lengths with orange spray painted *x*'s to facilitate immediate digging of the post holes. There was a work table set up on sawhorses, a cluster of tools topped with a circular saw, pre-made curved forms, and a cooler loaded with ice, waters, and soda. She was prepared for everything – everything except Cal.

"Let's get started," she said.

The fence project went well, for the most part. Tracy had planned for everything she could: drying times of the Quikcrete; swooping patterns to make the fence transition to gates (one that opened onto Deb's backyard, one that opened to the side by the driveway), and to make the fence a little prettier, a little more decorative (and to make it seem less enclosed, more friendly). Almost everything was done the first day, and the rest Tracy could finish herself. Tracy ordered pizzas for lunch, and Deb didn't even have to be asked over, but when she started in on Ian, Tracy stopped her. "He's seventeen, Deb."

The only other issue was also with Ian. She let Smoke and Red out a few times, after the posts were set, and the dogs and the guys all had fun together. She brought Stella out on a leash to do her business, but had told the guys she wasn't friendly and to ignore her. Everyone listened, it seemed. By afternoon, they were working around the back of the fence, near the lot line with Deborah's yard, so she tied the pits on their lines, and asked the guys if they were comfortable if she let Stella out on the porch. They all said sure. Before she did, she told them one more time that Stella didn't like strangers, but she'd ignore them, if they ignored her. She'd stay on the porch or the patio and give them plenty of room; she didn't want to meet them, so don't approach her, just respect her space. And she probably did look at Ian a little long when she said this, just because he was a teenager, and they could be a little impulsive. She let the dogs out. They all kept working, attaching the fencing panels, trimming the bottoms as they needed, checking the levels as they continued around the posts. As they turned the corner on the last side, nearest the garage, Tracy noticed it was just her and Cal and Luke; Ian had disappeared. As she looked around the edge of the panel for him, she saw him approaching Stella, where she was laying on the brick patio, in a square of shade made from the new fence. Her head was low, her eyes were locked on Ian, and her body tensed.

"Ian," Tracy yelled, "get away from her!" Luke whipped his head around to see his cousin crouching down with his hand held out.

Stella got up slowly and moved away from Ian, up onto the wooden porch, on the garage side, far away from Ian's overture. Ian came trotting back.

"I told you she doesn't like new people," Tracy said angrily when Ian rejoined them. Luke took Ian's baseball cap off and smacked him with it.

"Sorry, I love dogs," Ian said sheepishly, and picked up the decking nails, hanging his head. "I just wanted to make friends." About twenty minutes later, when they were all grabbing waters from the coolers, about twenty feet from Stella's new spot on the porch, Ian looked at her and made a kissy sound, and said, "Hey Stella, hey beautiful girl..." Stella locked eyes with him, and turned her head away, looking at the crumbling brick of the house, refusing to acknowledge him. Luke hooted and smacked Ian on the back.

"That is one lady, little cousin, who has no interest in you at all," and they went back to work. As Cal was attaching the gate mechanism along the driveway side, and Luke was trimming the gate panel, Tracy turned back toward the house just in time to see Ian again in front of Stella, his hand out, and this time Stella circled her large square head on the heavy neck (and it was anything but slow). Tracy heard the loud snap of the dog's jaws. She ran.

Ian was backing away, his mouth open. Tracy grabbed his shoulders, his young, tan and sweaty shoulders and turned him around, expecting to see his hand spurting blood, or the white glare of bone. He was intact. She turned to Stella, who had settled her giant head back down between her meaty paws, her eyes open and fixed on the pair.

"Stella! No!" Tracy yelled. "Bad dog!" She leapt the stairs, two at a time onto the porch. By this time, Luke had come running, and was standing with Ian; Cal had straightened up next to the gate, still holding the cross-piece, looking unsure what to do next. Tracy grabbed Stella's collar roughly. "Inside!" Her heart was racing. She made sure the screen door was closed and returned to Ian and Luke, taking the younger man's hand, inspecting it all over again.

"She didn't touch me," he said, his voice quiet. "It was just a snap." Tracy exhaled; she hadn't realized she been holding her breath.

"Are you OK?" As Tracy was asking this, Luke said, "She told you to stay away."

"I know, I know..." Ian answered. "It's OK, I mean, I'm OK, it's fine." And he was already reverting to his teenaged swaggering self, his I'm-fine-it's-just-a-dog-I-wasn't-really-scared self.

"I meant Stella," Luke said, and Ian turned to him. "That dog did every-thing she could do to tell you to stay away and you didn't listen. That snap was your last warning."

Stella was standing inside the screen door, watching them all.

Luke dropped Ian off at his house and went to meet Cal for a beer. When Luke had asked, as they were leaving Tracy's, Cal looked back over his shoulder and said, "Not Salty's," so they ended up at Club 23, outside of town. Club 23 was the place Cal had had his first beer. At thirteen, he got his first job, de-tassling corn, and when he got that initial paycheck, his father took him there, and bought him a beer, tapping the bottle neck lightly with his own, congratulating him on two weeks of hard work. Cal was still dirt- and dust-covered from his shift, but the beer tasted good and cold at first, although by the second sip he was beginning to wonder what it was about beer that made people like it so much. It was the same thing he'd thought about coffee when his mom had finally let him drink it, but he'd kept drinking it until he liked the taste just fine and he figured he'd do the same with beer.

Club 23 hadn't changed much over those twenty some years: a long bar, carpeting of various colors because parts of it had been replaced at different times, as needed. The light over the bar, and the one hanging over the pool table in back, were freebies from beer and liquor distributors, advertising their products; the colored plastic mottled to look like stained glass, but thin and chipped around the corners, hanging on cord wrapped in black electrical tape, blanketed with years of dust.

Cal was sitting at the end of the long bar, around the curve, when Luke walked in. He was already on his second beer, a can of PBR. Luke ordered a Leinie's Red in a bottle.

"I was going to buy you a beer for helping me out," Luke said, nodding in the direction of Cal's can.

"I got paid too, little brother." Since Cal's father had married Luke's mother, they got a kick out of calling each other brother, although no one else seemed to think of them this way; certainly Cal's sister didn't. She still thought of Luke as an ex-con and kept her kids away from him, as if he was dangerous, or his damaged reputation would somehow attach itself to her. At the wedding last fall, she'd barely acknowledged her stepmother ("you mean Dad's *new wife*," she'd corrected Cal) and left as soon as the cake was cut. It's true that Cal's dad and Luke's mom were an odd pairing in some ways – Cal's dad had never quite recovered his swagger after the muffler plant closed down and he lost his foreman position, and Luke's mom bragged a little too much about her cosmetology degree – but they seemed to make each other happy.

"Bourbon?" Luke asked Cal, and the bartender came towards them with two shot glasses and the bottle of Beam. After Cal's first semester of college at UW-Stout, when he'd first grown a beard and got his fake ID, he'd come to Club 23 with his high school friends that Christmas break, and drank beer and shots, smoked too many cigarettes, and puked all over this long bar top. The bartender then – maybe the same bartender as now – had simply started mopping up the sick with a bar rag and jerked his head in the direction of the door. Cal had taken it outside, puked some more, come back in for some water, then slept in his car until he sobered up enough to drive. Luke was talking about Tracy.

"I forgot how... efficient she is," he was saying.

"Efficient," Cal said.

"Don't you think that's sexy?" Luke was asking, as he turned on the swivel, high-backed bar stool to look directly at Cal.

"Was Ian OK?" Cal asked.

"Sure, he was fine. I think he learned something."

"That woulda scared the shit out of me," Cal said, and took another gulp of his beer.

"That was all Ian's fault," Luke said. "You know that, right?"

"Yeah, just, that's a big dog."

"It's just a dog, and it just wanted to be left alone. Tracy told him. Then the dog told him. That kid just doesn't listen, thinks all the girls are charmed by him," Luke smiled, finished his bottle and set it loudly on the bar, and nodded at the bartender who brought him another.

"Sounds like someone else I know," Cal said.

"Yup." Luke grinned showing his slightly crooked teeth. "And I hope Ian doesn't have to go to jail to learn that he's not smarter or more special than anyone else." Luke's troubles had cost him a scholarship to the Milwaukee School of Engineering, and who knows what else. He was doing fine, able to get work now, thanks to his old boss, and people like Tracy and others willing to give him the benefit of the doubt and a second chance. He'd probably never be able to catch up to where he would have been if he hadn't gotten cocky, and started stealing tools from the job site, then small machines, and finally parts from the larger earth-moving equipment and selling them on the side. When he sold what he thought was an abandoned bulldozer from the back pole building, a machine that hadn't been used in years, covered with a pile of lumber and sheeting, something he thought no one would notice or miss, he'd finally gone too far. The next morning, the cops were already there when he showed up at work. His boss was talking to them, and when Luke walked up, his lanky sure-footed walk stopped, and everybody knew who to talk to.

"Tracy sure looked surprised to see me," Cal said, turning toward Luke. He remembered how Luke had called him and asked if he wanted to make some extra cash on a Saturday. *Sure,* Cal had said. Tracy wasn't returning his calls, and he was between jobs right now anyway. Cal did a little bit of everything: restoring old houses, salvage and restoration, masonry, building, roofing. When Luke told him what the job was, Cal'd laughed. *Well, that's one way to see her*, he'd said.

Tracy had disappeared pretty quickly on him after that night they went to the park for the ball game; she'd clearly wanted him then, maybe even the next day. They'd had fun, Cal thought; she'd met his nephew, his sister and her husband, and on the porch, she'd been a little frantic. Cal didn't want her to do anything she'd regret, didn't want her to sleep with him and then just drop him, something he'd heard she did sometimes. Luke knew her from the tree-cutting business with her ex, and had told him that that guy – Greg – had cheated on her and she'd found out and just walked out one day, out of the house and out of the business. Cal had known lots of women who'd found out their boyfriends or husbands had been cheating, but he hadn't known of any women who'd just walked out like that, just left everything.

He hadn't told Tracy that he knew about Greg, what happened. He figured there was lots of time for those conversations as they got to know each other better. He'd spent the better part of a year trying to get to know her – making small talk when they happened to run into each other, buying her a no-pressure beer at Salty's, then leaving so she wouldn't feel like he was coming on too strong. His sister had told him about Tracy when she'd started working at the school, told him that maybe here was a girl for him. A local girl who had left then come back; was from a good family, who knew how to do things, who knew how to talk to people, who got along with everyone.

Cal hadn't really dated anyone seriously since high school, if high school dating can be considered serious at all. He knew his sister worried about him, wanted him to settle down and find a nice girl. Since his high school girlfriend dumped him senior year when she went off to Martin Luther to devote herself to her teaching degree and her calling, he hadn't been interested in 'nice girls' at all. The only 'nice girl' he'd known had dropped him before he could tell her he'd wait, that he'd follow her, that he'd be happy to support her in her calling. Maybe Tracy was the nice girl he was looking for. Cal had been trying really hard to be the kind of nice guy a nice girl might want in her life.

"You gonna call her?" Luke asked, shooting his second whiskey.

"Probably," Cal answered, noncommittal and not looking at Luke.

"Probably?" Luke asked, incredulous. "Why 'probably'? Why not 'definitely'? What's wrong with you?"

"I don't know little brother..." Cal slowed his reply. "That thing with Ian kind of freaked me out." The only change at Club 23 seemed to be one of those new digital juke boxes, hung on the back wall behind the pool table, the kind connected to the internet, where a person could find and play any kind of music he wanted, if he was willing to pay. Cal put a five on the bar and signaled the bartender. "Could we get some singles? How about some music?" he asked Luke.

"Well, Tracy's not my boss anymore, big brother, and I'll tell you, I think a woman who can rebuild her own house, handle a circle saw, and handle a dog like that is very sexy. If you're out, I'm in," and he clinked his bottle neck against Cal's PBR can, where it made no sound.

"You're kidding."

"No, big brother, I am not kidding," Luke answered.

"Isn't she a little old for you?" Cal asked.

"What's a few years?" Luke said, and he looked serious. "Besides – she looks damn good." Cal was quiet, trying to figure out if Luke was taunting him, egging him on to do what even Cal knew he should do – call Tracy again – or if he was giving him fair warning. "I'm going to play some music, and then I'm going to take a squirt, and then we're going to play some darts," and Luke moved back to the jukebox.

They played darts and Cal lost, as he always did. Just as Luke was closing at cricket, Ronnie McDowell's "Older Women" came on the jukebox. "You've got a month to make your move, big brother. Or I make mine."

Part Two: July

Appointments

The Monday after the holiday weekend, Lucy made an appointment for Tracy. She set it up with Dr. Larsen instead of Dr. Schulz. Dr. Larsen was a little younger and new to the practice, but seemed to have a better rapport with some of the bigger dogs. Dr. Schulz was a sweetie, but more of a cat man, a small dog man. Lucy could imagine him trying to win Stella over with baby talk, getting down on the floor with her, eye to eye. Even after meeting Stella that first time, Lucy had known this was exactly the wrong approach. Since spending more time with the dog yesterday, she was sure of it. After hanging up the phone with Tracy, she entered the appointment into the computer, and added a few notes: *3 dogs, large breed, rescue. Behavioral history unknown; veterinary history unknown.* After deliberating for a moment, she added, *basket muzzle Stella (mastiff).* She double checked the staff schedule for that day. The tech would be Sarah; Donna, the part-time receptionist, would be there to cover the front desk, if Lucy needed to help Tracy wrangle the dogs, or hold a leash, or walk them through the new strange environment of the vet office, which would smell like antiseptic and animal fear. She reserved the large exam room. As she was saving the changes, Dr. Schulz came out of the nearest exam room, covered with tufts of fur from the Persian he'd just examined, his black multi-pleated pants drowning his skinny ankles. He was whistling.

Lucy had started working at the vet clinic about eight years ago when their last receptionist had up and quit. The vet tech at the time had called her. Dr. Schulz had recommended her to clients who were looking for training and behavioral work. They'd let her keep her business cards for *Pawsitive Solutions* on the front desk, and through them, she'd been able to keep a steady rotation of Manners I & II classes, Agility classes, and a recently added Tricks class (for pet people who wanted to impress the neighbors).

She and Carla had cordoned off a large yard area for her dog classes (the agility equipment took up a lot of room) which ran from April to October. They sometimes had invitationals to show off the dogs' agility skills, or coursing trials. It was all for fun, but people loved to show off their dogs, meet other dog people, and she usually got a few new clients out of it.

What Lucy really loved was working with the difficult dogs: the scared, anxious, and aggressive dogs. Most of the 'difficult' dogs were all three at once. Most of the people who had these dogs had the best of intentions, but couldn't see how they were inadvertently making their animals worse. They'd start by trying to give all the love and affection they could, and ended up reinforcing the behaviors they wanted to curtail. For these dogs, Lucy insisted on two assessments before they even started work: one at the dog's home and one on neutral territory – Lucy's training field, or a park or trail. Lucy wasn't parochial; she'd try just about any approach or method to reach a dog, as long as it didn't do any further damage to the animal.

These assessment visits could go any number of ways, but most often they went one way. At the home visit, the dog's person did a lot of talking. That's what people do: they narrate to explain things in a way that makes sense to them. When confronted with gaps, with unknowables, people tried to fill in the gaping maw. And these dogs, who acted in strange and unpredictable ways – snapping and charging, growling, guarding food or toys, scaring people they should love – were the perfect vessel for stories. People with rescue dogs did this really well. Lucy had heard these people take just a few details and stitch together a whole epic, a great American novel worthy of a Pulitzer, all to explain why the animal they loved so much behaved in such unloveable ways. But as their person is talking, Lucy watches the dog. She sees how the dog responds, not how the person would explain the dog. That's really what she's come to see anyway.

So many dogs described as aggressive – a lot of the big ones – weren't; so many little dogs were, but weren't described that way. She saw the dogs who were fearful, bark and back away. She saw the dogs who weren't afraid, but knew their people were, and responded only to that. She heard the people saying *Coco likes this*…and Coco's whale eyes were begging her person to please stop. During this first visit, she usually just observed, took notes, watched the dog and its people in their space. Only if there were kids, or a safety issue, did she feel compelled to step in. Then they'd make a plan:

build the dog's confidence, use repetition and reward, or reconfigure the household to meet the dog's and people's needs.

After the fence was up, after the scare with Ian, Tracy called Lucy. She'd been spooked by the snap, and had Lucy's card affixed to the fridge. Lucy was at home on her Wednesday off (the first of July) and was able to go over that afternoon. She pulled into the drive and noticed the new green of the wooden fence in the backyard; the new gate that spanned the brick opening on the front porch, all the changes Tracy had made for the dogs. Tracy was waiting in the driveway. The pits were just inside the back fence gate, wagging their tails. Stella was nowhere to be seen.

Lucy explained that mainly she wanted to see the dogs at their home, see how they behaved with Tracy, with each other, with a new person. They wouldn't be doing any training that afternoon, but they'd talk and by the end of the hour, Lucy would have some ideas for how to proceed, and what the dogs' needs were.

"OK," Tracy said. "How do we start?"

"Well, I'm going to sit down at the patio table and you're going to let Stella out," Lucy answered. Tracy started toward the back door, where Lucy could make out the silhouette of the big dog through the screen. As Tracy reached for the leash hanging alongside the door, Lucy said, "Off leash." Tracy hesitated then opened the door. Stella came slowly down the steps.

"Now just come back and sit next to me and we'll talk."

Tracy joined Lucy at the patio table, a small two-top of metal mesh. Usually it wasn't occupied until later in the day when Deb would make her way over, carrying a too-full wine glass. Tracy would have her own beer, and open a bag of chips, or maybe bring out a bag of grapes or cherries, trying to get something into her neighbor's stomach along with the alcohol. (Deb would take a few handfuls, out of politeness, but she seemed to know what Tracy was up to.) After circling the visitor for a few rubdowns, the pits would lay down in the table's shade. They did that now, on their sides, beneath Tracy's swinging leg, crossed right over left, and Lucy's solidly-planted feet, her skin tan in her athletic sandals. Stella stayed even alongside Tracy; Lucy ignored her and talked to Tracy.

After a minute or two of standing very still beside Tracy, Stella wandered a wide arc behind Lucy, approached the back of her neck and began to sniff her hair, big sniffs that fluffed Lucy's curly, chin-length hair, snuffling it out in the mid-afternoon heat.

"Did you cut your hair?" Tracy asked.

"It's just the humidity," Lucy laughed. "It gets shorter and shorter through the summer."

"I always wanted curly hair. Used to spend hours trying to curl it. And it'd fall flat again in minutes," Tracy said.

"Every straight-haired girl wants curly. Every curly-haired girl wants straight," Lucy said, staying still while Stella's hot breath made new cowlicks. "Same old story. OK, tell me about the snap."

As Tracy started to tell the story, she became visibly upset. Stella noticed before Lucy did, and left her newly found interest in the back of Lucy's neck to lay her boxy head in her person's lap, wagging her long tail, making low, singing noises in her throat.

Turned out Stella was a talker. It was a surprise to Tracy at first, but once they had gotten home after their three day road trip, each day brought a new vocalization. In the morning, Stella would rest her whole head on Tracy in bed, singing her morning song. She'd stretch and yawn, a series of throaty moans. When she'd settle down to bed at night, after circling her spot in the bed three times, she'd grunt and groan, and let out her loud exhale, jowls flapping, before falling to sleep. The dog dreamed deeply, twitching and yipping, waking Tracy until she'd nudge her and say her name, and the dog would quiet. She snored, a steady heartbeat of a sound that had become Tracy's sleep machine. Stella had a noise when it was getting close to feeding time and she didn't think Tracy was paying enough attention to the clock. She had a noise when Tracy was in the bathroom with the door closed too long. And although she didn't bark, she chuffed like a tiger when she wanted to alert Tracy to a potential danger. Tracy would be having coffee on the front porch with Stella at her feet. Tracy'd hear the sound, a quick inhale-exhale of breath, and know the mailman was coming up the walk. It was why she had installed the gate out front. As long as whoever it was stayed on that side of the barrier, all Stella would do was stand alert by Tracy's side and chuff.

Tracy told Lucy all this and more about her life with the dogs. But when Lucy asked about the dogs' pasts, Tracy's most common answer was "I don't know." She told Lucy her brother had had the dogs for a few months before he'd died, maybe four, no more than six, and that he'd lived out in the woods, pretty isolated, although there were a few people they were friendly with. She told her all she'd learned from Sam – that Smoke had had a litter of pups, that Red was a bait dog, that Stella had been returned to the shelter multiple times.

Lucy thought Tracy's not knowing the dogs' stories was probably a good thing; the way she said *bait dog* made it seem like she didn't really know what that meant. Lucy had felt all the scars on Red, noted her small size, the way she was clearly the most submissive, and thought about what that all meant.

She remembered the first time Carla had gotten her up and riding a horse, an Arabian they were boarding all those years ago in Iowa, and how she hadn't had a clue about what she was doing. She'd told Carla this as they were leaving the paddock and moving from a slow walk into a little canter. Her body caught the rhythm of the body underneath her and automatically responded, moving in its own answering rhythm.

"What do I do now?" she'd called ahead to Carla, a little anxious, her hands on the reins. Some low-hanging tree branches obscured all but the high tail and back legs of Carla's horse in front of her. Carla had laughed and said something, but Lucy couldn't make it out. They'd kept riding. Later, she'd told Carla that she didn't know what she'd been doing – she'd never ridden before.

"That's why you did so well," Carla had said. "You had no time to think." Lucy had looked uncertain, but Carla was right. She wasn't thinking or worrying about what she should do, if she was riding the right way, or where her leg should be, or her posture, or the horse's gait. She was just riding.

Tracy was just figuring out things on her own, too – not knowing what "bait dog" meant, or what Red had been through. It meant she didn't have those pictures in her head every time she reached for the little dog, every time she hooked up the leash to the collar. (The first time she'd put the collar on the dog, she instinctively made it loose enough so that it didn't rub against all the scars.)

For the second half of the assessment, they walked around the house. Stella would stand in doorways, but Lucy moved assertively, told the dog "Go" in a firm voice and the dog did. Smoke and Red followed Stella's lead in everything. After a few minutes of moving around the house, the two pits curled up on the couch. Lucy sat down between them, but when they tried to crawl closer to her, she told them "No," and they respected her space. Stella laid down on the floor across from Lucy, crossed her front paws, and rested her head on top of them. The dogs had responded immediately to most commands: go, sit, stay, down.

"Well," Lucy said, "I have some ideas, but what are your concerns? How can I help you?"

"Well," Tracy said, standing in the doorway to the bedroom. "I..."

"Sit down," Lucy said, waiting for Tracy to find a chair. "Tell me how I can make your life with the dogs easier."

"Oh!" Tracy exclaimed and Stella looked up at her. "I'd like to be able to walk them a little less frantically."

"That's easy," Lucy answered. "Smoke and Red need some leash training – we'd talked about that before. And I think you might want to walk them separately from Stella. More time consuming but it'll be easier on you."

"OK." Tracy paused. "Stella's aggression."

"I'm not sure that's what I'd call it. She's reserved but it's not like she's moving aggressively towards people. The situation you described with that boy sounds like a defensive move," Lucy explained. "Now, that doesn't mean she couldn't be dangerous."

"Dangerous?"

"Yes. If she was cornered and couldn't move away. Or – and I think this is the biggest issue – if she thought you were in danger, she could respond very strongly to protect you." Lucy wanted to be very clear with Tracy. She didn't think Stella would just go after people, but if someone bothered Tracy, Stella could be a deadly weapon.

Tracy was tearing up again, thinking about Aaron, thinking about Stella and Aaron, and now about Stella and her. The evening they'd gotten home from Idaho (after the surprise meeting with Deb, and taking the dogs for a quick and exasperating walk around the block, feeding them, and unloading the van), she'd locked up the house and turned on a scalding hot shower. With her eyes shut, the water on full blast, she was on her second shampoo, letting the suds run down her skin and collect at the bottom of the tub (where the drain always ran a little slow), when she felt something graze the back of her naked ass cheek. Startled, she opened her eyes under the hot spray, and turned around to see Stella, half in the shower, front paws submerged in the wasted water, misted droplets caught in folds of skin and fur and jowls. Stella looked up at her, big eyes and whites showing. Tracy hunkered down in the big tub, and held the dog to her wet and once-clean body. Stella was shaking.

Tracy was shaken by what Lucy had said. She didn't know what to do with Lucy's warning, how to assimilate this information about this dog she loved, how to integrate this idea about Stella as "dangerous" with the Stella she knew. On walks, sometimes a car would slow to ask about the dog, and Stella would swing her big head toward the rolled down window. If the person asking started to open the door, or approach, she'd step in front of Tracy. Once, a man had stumbled too close, after Tracy tried to signal he should keep his distance, but the big dog just rolled her shoulders forward and dropped her head. Tracy couldn't always read this canine body language, but that man could. As he veered a wide arc, she heard him say under his breath, "Nobody's gonna fuck with you."

Lucy tried to reassure her; she told her they'd use classical conditioning techniques to de-sensitize Stella to certain situations; that there were various ways to control environments and introduce Stella to people to make every-one safer. On the way out, Lucy approved of the fence, touching Stella ever so lightly on the tip of her nose with the tip of her finger. Stella's tail wagged.

"This weekend's the Fourth of July," Lucy said, her hand on the gate. The dogs were busy sniffing around the yard.

"Oh yes," Tracy said, "Happy Fourth."

"You too, but I meant the dogs, the fireworks…"

"The fireworks?" Tracy asked, cocking her head to the side, peering at Lucy.

"You really don't know dogs… lots of dogs are bothered by fireworks. Some really freak out," Lucy said. "Keep the dogs inside. They could easily go over the fence."

"Really? Over the fence?" Tracy looked at her beautiful fence, where she'd sawed out portions of the center panels in rounded arcs to make it look less like a compound, less like a prison fence, but now realized that that had maybe been a mistake. She'd planned to hang a few plants from the posts to make it more inviting.

"Well, I don't think they'd jump it on their own, but fireworks make some dogs go crazy. You should just see how they are. And don't leave them out here on their own."

Tracy looked over at the dogs. Stella was hunkered down at the far edge of the yard by the neighbors, and when Smoke meandered over, she chased her away, a lunge paired with a little growl. Smoke ran over to Tracy and Lucy, her thin tail between her legs.

"What's she got there?" Lucy asked.

"I don't know," Tracy said and they both walked over to where Stella had nosed a tiny nest of dry grass and grey fur away from a hole in the yard. In the hole, there was a tangle of pink-grey bodies writhing. Stella's big nose was resting right next to the hole, sniffing deeply.

"A rabbit's nest," Lucy whispered, and Tracy said low, "Stella, no..." Stella looked up at her. Lucy put her hand on her arm. "These dogs don't have much of a prey drive."

"Prey drive?" Tracy asked, looking at Lucy, looking down at big Stella watching her rabbits, the two pits keeping their distance.

"She's all protection, your girl. Now those two," and she pointed to the other dogs across the yard, "they'd like those babies for breakfast, but Stella here," and Lucy hunkered down next to the big dog, companionably, but not touching her, "she's keeping them safe." Tracy stooped down too, folding herself over her knees. "Don't forget that. Don't get caught up in your head about her."

Tracy thought about the night Deb had stumbled on the brick patio and fallen, and Stella had moved quickly from the porch, and had started nuzzling the back of her neck. Deb and Stella had still been wary of each other, giving each other plenty of room. But in her drunkenness, inhibitions lowered, Deb had reached up and grabbed Stella's neck, using the dog's body and braced legs to pull herself up. And Stella had stood there, then *assisted*, the dog's plodding steps timed to the drunken neighbor's pace. It had happened before Tracy could get there herself. Deb'd moved away then, making for her house, not turning back toward Tracy, steadying herself all the while on Stella. In the glow from the porch flood light, and a sliver of moon, Tracy thought she saw blood. Stella stood at the lot line until Tracy joined her. They both watched until their neighbor reached her house, listened to the back door slam shut. Stella whined and turned back toward the house.

Now Tracy smiled across the rabbit's nest at Lucy, while Stella's eyes made a three-point path from Tracy to the kits to Lucy.

"And don't forget to make a vet appointment. Call tomorrow. I'll be there."

Deb came over that night, a few hours after Lucy left. For once, Tracy joined her in finishing a bottle and opened another. Deb said the fence looked good. Deb said the fence crew looked good. Tracy had to agree. She'd been thankful for her wayward neighbor's over-the-top response when the guys had shed their t-shirts because it had likely hidden hers. She hadn't been around that many young, shirtless men since the tree-trimming crew at Shade. Cal looked good, the way men who worked with their hands often and easily, looked: lean and muscled with veins that stood up in relief on their forearms. He was burnished all over. The tan even dipped down below the waist of his jeans when he bent over to pick up another bag of concrete or sink the shovel into the edge of the machine-dug post hole. It had been a hot day and Tracy wanted to guard against dehydration, but that hadn't been the only reason she'd been glad for the iced-down bottles of water she kept drinking.

Even though at first she'd been pissed that Luke had shown up with Cal unannounced, all pretended innocence, she liked that they were friends and liked seeing them together, their easy friendship, the constant joking. In a way, knowing that Luke approved of Cal was sort of a recommendation. And one she valued. As the day wore on, she and Cal worked together well. Even at that dicey moment with Stella, they'd been across from each other, hanging the gate at the driveway, alternating tools, speaking in half-sentences and nods. When she'd blown the bangs out of her eyes for about the fifth time, he'd braced the gate on his knee and reached over to push the bangs out of her face, hooking them behind her ear. She'd just been thinking about leaning her cheek into the palm of his hand when she'd caught the movement of Ian approaching Stella out of the corner of her eye.

The fireflies were coming out, lighting their tiny lights in the fenced-in backyard, so quick that by the time Tracy registered them, their light was already gone. She remembered a party in high school, sitting on the edge of a corn field watching the fireflies while she pretended to smoke a cigarette she'd bummed. She didn't know how to inhale, so she'd just puff and puff every once in a while, keeping the cherry going. A firefly, confused, landed on her hand, drawn to the glowing ember of her cigarette, firing its own little engine, its lantern of desire. She put the cigarette out, afraid the firefly would kill itself, drawn to the false female in her hand.

"You know what I like about that Cal?" Deb was starting to slur.

"What Deb?"

"Chest hair. What is it with guys these days and the no-chest-hair thing?" A definite slur. Deb was holding her wine glass by the stem and didn't look to have too steady of a grip on it. Tracy resisted the urge to take it from her, set it down, and get her a water. Besides, she had a point about the chest hair. Somewhere along the line, younger men had decided to do something about that – were they waxing it? Shaving it? Had men started to evolve beyond chest hair and grow naturally hairless? Tracy wasn't sure what the evolutionary point of chest hair was anyway, but aesthetically she appreciated it. Cal's was dark, with little flecks of grey, not unlike his beard. He seemed to favor crew neck t-shirts, but even then there'd be a curl or two above the collar. When he took his shirt off, he had a nice wide-based triangle, spreading onto his pecs, and then that little line that trailed down his navel and into his jeans.

"I'm going to call him," she said, thinking about where that line led.

"Good girl!" Deb cheered, toasting Tracy then tottering back home.

Round Two

Saturday night and Cal was on his way to pick up Tracy. He'd told Luke he'd have to back off because technically they had a date, even if she'd called him. Luke laughed but agreed that that was close enough. They were going to the next town over, to the annual Fourth of July weekend festival, even though Saturday fell on the third. There was live music, a street dance, a grilling competition, and fireworks. Cal had gone the last couple of years, but not with a date, so wasn't sure if he should dress differently. He'd settled on a pair of dark wash jeans and a clean t-shirt. It looked like Tracy had a made a similar decision, but he noticed she was wearing sandals with a little heel, instead of her sneakers, and that her toenails were painted pink. She might have been wearing a bit of lip gloss. He picked her up in his work truck, but he'd emptied the back of loose tools, cleaned the cab of trash, and hung a new air freshener shaped like a tiny pine tree. He tuned the radio to the classic rock station instead of the regular NPR talk radio he usually listened to.

"Are you a dancer?" she asked him on the drive over, a quick ten minutes.

"I've been known to dance," he said, "after a couple of beers..." One of the bands played a mix of their own stuff and covers of 80s and 90s tunes, so there were plenty of songs that both he and Tracy knew that reminded them of when they were young. Lately Cal had been feeling old – well, older, and he wasn't sure how he felt about that.

His nephew was starting eighth grade next year, and he thought he'd detected a few mustache hairs on his upper lip, growing darker and thicker. The poor kid's voice was changing, so that half the time when Cal called on the phone he got confused about who he was talking to, and either thought he had the wrong number or that he was talking to his brother-in-law.

He remembered his own eighth grade year as full of embarrassment and wonder. Mostly he remembered Mrs. Erickson's language arts class and the green blackboards that rimmed the room; the books they had to read and discuss. He never knew what he was supposed to say, even though he'd done all the reading, usually multiple times. Mrs. Erickson always looked at him, vaguely disappointed. But the worst was diagramming sentences. He was petrified of Fridays, the diagramming-sentences days and it seemed like on those days, Mrs. Erickson took a particular dislike to him, calling him in front of the class to demonstrate his inadequacy. Every part of the sentence went somewhere. The whole board would be covered with blanks and slanted lines, but no matter how hard Cal tried to make every part go somewhere, he could never get them all to fit.

Cal could dance, and they did have fun, and they both felt young, and when Cal slowed to turn off back to Tracy's house, she said that she wouldn't mind going back to his place. She did find out where that narrow line of hair on his belly led. Tracy had already figured out that Cal wasn't quite the nice guy he was pretending to be. And by the way Tracy used her teeth, Cal knew she wasn't quite the nice girl he thought she was.

Tracy woke up to the smell of coffee and bakery and wasn't sure where she was. The ceilings were high, stamped tin, and the tall windows let in morning light and squares of sky that fell on a condom wrapper on the floor. Cal was walking towards her with two coffees in paper cups, barefoot.

"I got you a mocha, hope that's alright."

He sat down on the edge of the bed. She sat up, still naked, not bothering to pull the sheet up to cover anything. Cal had spent a few minutes looking at her before he went downstairs for the coffee, seeing in greater detail what had been half-hidden in dim light the night before. Maybe Tracy wasn't the kind of woman who would immediately turn heads, but he liked her body. Her breasts were medium-sized with large brown nipples, like silver dollars. He could see a scar on her stomach from an appendectomy but, other than that, it was mostly smooth, curving in a little at the waist, and then out to a nice-sized ass, one that he enjoyed the memory of cupping in his hands last night. She leaned over for her coffee.

"Thanks." Tracy could tell he was trying not to look too obviously, staring mostly into his coffee as he blew on it. She was fully exposed, one leg stretched out in front of her, one knee bent. "These sheets are..."

"Um, yeah, I didn't know we'd be coming back here."

The sheets were black and scratchy, definitely cheap. Other than this unfortunate choice, his place was nice – one of those apartments in the small downtown, above one of the stores, probably the coffee shop and bakery that catered to the summer people, in the brick block, historic. It was like a loft – open rooms, exposed beams, original woodwork in various stages of restoration.

"This your place?" she asked.

"Yeah, I own the building, rent out the downstairs. I've been restoring it, slowly."

"It's beautiful, but... you haven't quite gotten to the bedroom." Tracy laughed. They were on a box spring and mattress on the floor, with black sheets of cheap poly, stiff with wear, unwashed.

"OK. This is gross, but I kind of just use sheets for about a month, then throw them out and buy a new set." Cal hung his head. It's something he'd done since college, he couldn't explain why. He had a washing machine and dryer. He washed his clothes regularly, cared about the quality of his towels, but something about bedding, about buying bedding and washing it, stank of adulthood to him, so he held onto this practice like some sort of superstition, like a baseball player with lucky socks. "Um, unfortunately, you came over near the end of the cycle."

He gave Tracy a tour, showing her his latest project: the kitchen. He'd poured concrete countertops, installed new appliances, and utilized repurposed industrial materials where he could: some diamond plate as a backsplash, some old metal molds affixed above the cabinets. The table was beautiful, a mismatch of reclaimed wood he was in the process of sanding soft to the touch before he'd treat it with beeswax, keeping the rough edges of the planks, the wood's natural knots and flaws. The chairs were old and industrial, blued metal with wood seats. Here and there were a few large stones piled around the room, extras he'd claimed from jobs he'd worked. One had a trilobite fossil perfectly revealed, the sandstone pale and crumbly. One was a large block of red granite from a local quarry with three inset cylinders drilled into it where a quarry worker would have dropped dynamite to blow apart the rock. One was flat and square, the grey slate like stacked paper or envelopes, sleeves stacked and ready to be split apart into its own flat planes. Cal didn't know what he'd end up doing with these collections of stone, but he liked having them around – their shapes and colors, their roughness and smoothness.

After their coffee and the tour, Tracy leaned over and kissed him again, pushing her hands up under his soft t-shirt, leading him back to the sad bedroom.

"Don't you have to get home?" he said. "The dogs?"

"Deborah's taking care of them," she murmured, her mouth hidden in his neck, his beard.

After, he'd asked who Deborah was. "My neighbor," Tracy said.

"Oh," Cal laughed, "Foxy Grandma."

"She calls you "Sexy Beardy,"" Tracy said. "Actually she has nicknames for all of you."

"Who's "all of you?" " Cal asked.

"Every man in town." Tracy said. "But she's especially fond of my fence crew. She's hoping I'll have some more work done very soon."

"Oh yeah? What's Luke's?"

"Cool Hand," but Cal looked confused. "You know, blue eyes..." but when Cal still didn't get it, she said, "Haven't you seen that movie with Paul Newman? Never mind."

"And Ian?"

"Jailbait," Tracy said.

When she'd told Deb she had a date with Cal, Deb had offered to check on the dogs that night so that Tracy wouldn't have to be back by any certain time. She'd added, if Tracy wasn't back in the morning, she'd come over and feed the girls and let them out – then she winked. Ever since Stella had come to Deb's rescue, the ice had been broken between them, and now the evening visits included all three dogs greeting their neighbor. Now Stella would lie at Deb's feet just as often as she laid at Tracy's. Deb had come over a few days after her fall, with a bruised cheek and a cut on her forehead. It had been for coffee in the morning. She'd sat in the chair and Stella had come right over, resting her head in Deb's lap. Deb kept her eyes on Stella.

"Thanks for your help the other night, Stella," and the dog's tail wagged. "And you too, Tracy." Tracy had started to say something but Deborah cut her off. "That was my daughter's birthday and it was a rough day for me. I had too much."

"I didn't know you had a daughter," Tracy said quietly, looking deeply into her coffee mug, as Deborah still looked only at the dog.

"Well, I don't really. I haven't been much of a mother to her. After her father, my first husband, died, I cuddled up with the bottle pretty good, and she's got no reason to forgive that. We don't talk." Stella had settled now at Deb's feet, leaning the full weight of her body against the older woman, and Deb was bracing herself, trying to keep her body and her chair upright.

"Look, Tracy, I know you check on me sometimes, and I appreciate it, but I don't want to talk about it. What I do want to say is that there are lots of ways to keep people away. And now you've got these dogs, and it makes me a little worried for you." She rested her hand on Stella's broad forehead, using her thin fingers to pet the still-soft fur between the dog's big eyes, soothing her. Stella's eyelids slowly drooped and closed. "That's all I wanted to say."

The Monday after the holiday, after her date with Cal, Tracy arrived at the vet office with Smoke and Red, already tangled in their leashes, nearly tripping her as they wound their way around her bare legs. When Lucy saw her, she jumped up from behind the desk, and went over to greet the dogs and calm them down. Red, in particular, was reacting to the new environment with abject terror, cowering and leaving a little trail of urine on the floor. Lucy started working her magic: talking in low tones, re-directing the dogs, offering a treat whenever they straightened up and relaxed their tails from between their legs. Stella had simply refused to get out of the car. Lucy laughed, talked to Donna, the other receptionist, filled her pockets with a fresh supply of liver treats, and headed back out with Tracy, linking arms, for round two. Tracy paled a little when she saw the basket muzzle in Lucy's hand. Lucy shushed her. "Trust me," she said.

Lucy was able to get Stella out of the car, but instead of heading back to the clinic's front doors, she led the wayward group around back to where the yard opened up to a wide field. They ran the dogs a little, then practiced some sits and stays, rewarding them with the treats, ambling Stella along, too. Stella knew every command Lucy gave her, even silent hand commands. Each dog did her business and took a long drink from the water pails behind the building. Lucy introduced Stella to the muzzle, setting it on her face and rewarding her for tolerating it with a liver treat a few times before she finally attached the straps and adjusted them. Tracy squinched up her face, but Lucy explained that it was just a precaution, and better safe than sorry. After brushing it with her big paws a few times, Stella didn't seem that bothered, and Lucy explained that although it looked bad, the dog could breathe and pant and drool just fine, a point made as the first, big plop of spittle fell from the wire cage to the grass.

When they entered the clinic, Red seemed calmer, Smoke just kept walking, and Lucy decided to handle Stella. Tracy was grateful for Lucy's help, yet again, especially when she saw the stricken look on the vet tech Sarah's face.

"OK," Lucy said, "first, let's get the weights."

In the back room, there was a large scale on the floor, only requiring the dogs to step up a few inches and either sit or stand immobile for a few seconds. The pits did pretty well, but Stella was immediately suspicious of the shiny metal object, its slight wobble under her feet. Lucy was patient, offering the tantalizing liver treats, but it still took several tries, with both Tracy and Lucy forming a cordon with their bodies to get her to stand still long enough to get a reading.

Dr. Larsen entered just as they were finally accomplishing this first task. Sarah had mainly been observing, and Lucy had been talking to her in the same low and steady voice she used to gentle the dogs, explaining that she'd handle Stella, who was a bit anxious, but didn't show it in the regular ways. Dr. Larsen heard the end of the lecture, Lucy telling Sarah to pretend she was back in high school, playing hard to get. "Just pretend there's no dog in the room," Lucy said.

"What dog?" Dr. Larsen said. "I don't see a dog." Tracy liked him immediately. His teeth were a little crooked, and he had a long forehead, a long nose. He was slim and tall, but not imposing. He sat down on the chair in the corner and let Smoke and Red come to him, which they did, immediately.

"So," he said, "you've gotten yourself some dogs."

Tracy didn't even know the exam had begun. She thought he was just petting the dogs, but he'd note things, and Sarah would write them down. Neither pit had been spayed – he couldn't find a scar, and he thought Smoke had had a least one litter. He thought Red was quite young, only two or three; Smoke maybe a little older, but not much. They seemed healthy, good weight, good coats, good musculature, and all that. They had no problem letting him look at their teeth and eyes and ears. They talked about titer testing, required vaccinations, heartworm preventatives, and concerns about ticks and Lyme's disease. Lucy would contribute to the conversation sometimes. Tracy would ask questions. In the end, she decided to have all three dogs get a combo vaccine and blood draws and to test for heartworm and Lyme's.

Dr. Larsen asked how the dogs handled the fireworks last night, and Tracy sighed. Smoke and Red had tried to hide under the bed. Red was little enough, but Smoke couldn't fit all the way so was only able to get her head and back end under, but her belly wouldn't fit. There was a silver curve showing most of the evening, quivering. Tracy sat next to her on the floor, slowly stroking the half-circle of visible dog. Stella was stoic as usual, but wouldn't eat, which was strange. Stella loved to eat just about anything. During the fireworks, when Tracy offered her the leftover crusts of her pizza, Stella just left them on the floor, but Tracy hadn't seen her pacing, or shaking, or startling at any of the loud noises.

"Some dogs don't show fear or anxiety in the ways we're used to seeing," Dr. Larsen explained. "They're introverts." He nodded at Stella who was sitting next to Tracy, and seemed oblivious to the vet's office and what was going on with the other dogs, but hadn't eaten the last few liver treats Lucy had given her. "Not eating might be how Stella shows anxiety."

Tracy was surprised by how both Smoke and Red just froze for the needles, and then when it was over, began wagging their tails and licking Dr. Larsen and Sarah's hands. Stella was a different story, though – she tolerated the exam, as long as Lucy and Tracy held her big head. Dr. Larsen could touch her behind the neck, feel her stomach and legs, stretch out her legs to check her hips. (He pronounced them "OK – not great, but not bad." When Tracy looked puzzled, Lucy said, "Hip dysplasia.".) He located the scar on her belly from when she was spayed. When he inserted the needle for the blood draw, she whipped her head out of their hands and locked eyes with him. When he inserted the thermometer into her rectum to take her temperature, she growled a low growl. "We're almost done Stella," he said, patting her hip, and she flicked her eyes up at Tracy. "OK," he said, "all done."

Lucy was still holding Stella's leash loosely, but Tracy let go of the dog's head. Stella swung around, lowered her head and pinned Dr. Larsen to the wall with her flat cranium, her forehead pressed against his crotch.

"Stella ... " he said. She chuffed. She lifted him a few inches, so that his toes were barely touching the floor, her eyes canted up and hard. She chuffed again and then lowered him back down, walked across the room to Tracy, laid down and crossed her paws, one atop the other, before resting her head on them. No one said anything until the dog settled and sighed.

"Well," Dr. Larsen said, red-faced.

Sarah was speechless.

"And that's why we have the muzzle," Lucy said, all business.

Sarah

A few hours later, Sarah found herself still smiling; smiling as she was weighing the Miller poodles, as she was checking the kidney function results for the Eckstrand's elderly, domestic shorthair, the corners of her mouth turning up. As she was placing the order for Heartgaard (ensuring there'd be plenty of refills at the various weights available for walk-ins), she was almost laughing, showing teeth. It was something about Dr. Larsen's toes barely touching the floor, his thick-soled shoes squeaking against the linoleum and the look on his face. On the drive home, she giggled a little, and by the time she was pulling into the garage, she laughed out loud.

She couldn't really blame the big dog, stripped of her normal methods of communication, locked into that small room, the indignity of the temperature-taking. And Dr. Larsen telling her he was almost done, smacking her on the rump, like she should just put up with it. She hadn't hurt him and she could have – it had just been a warning, but an effective one at that. In a strange way, Sarah admired the dog's restraint. Most dogs barked and yapped, expending huge amounts of energy to no end. Even though she would have been nervous working with that dog on her own, it was exactly that sort of animal and interaction that had made her want to be a vet.

Or at least that's what she'd taken to telling herself, in the way she'd taken to telling herself things, over the years, as things had not turned out for her, not the way she wanted. The story was that she'd wanted to be a vet ever since she was little; that she loved animals, loved caring for them. She'd ended up a vet tech and just barely. She was living at home with her mother and step-father who hovered, and asked too many times how she was feeling, if she was taking her medications, how her appointment went this week.

And so she pulled into the garage still laughing, but after she put the car into park, she could already see the light over the kitchen sink go on, her mother's face dimly lit through the glass, checking on her, always checking on her. She pulled the keys out of the ignition, grabbed her purse, and readied herself for a dinner with audible chewing and swallowing and too much silence before she could escape to her room. Escape from them.

Sarah had gotten good grades in high school, had taken extra science and summer enrichment classes, and left the next fall for college. But college wasn't what she'd thought. She'd picked a small school, certain that this would be an easier transition for her (smaller classes, more like what she was used to in her little town with teachers and friends who had known her since childhood who were careful with her particular quirks: her slight discomfort with the new, the too-loud, the strange, her lack of interest in the things normal kids seemed to be interested in). But that first day of orientation, she knew she'd made a terrible mistake.

She and all the other first-year students had sat around the dorm common room, and were supposed to tell a story that conveyed who they were. Sarah didn't know how to pick one story, how to encapsulate her life into a short tale about her brothers, her mother and father, the little two-story she grew up in; her parents' divorce, the way her older brother chose to live with their dad; how she and her younger brother went back and forth between their parents, always forgetting something or other they needed for school, missing clothes and homework and track uniforms. Or how quickly her mother married again and how quickly her father took that too-easy cue to opt out of being a father. Her dorm mates seemed to think this ice-breaker activity was easy, fun even; telling their stories, earning nicknames in the process, laughing and forming quick friendships, the beginnings of flirtations. Sarah slowly shrank backwards, disappearing to the bathroom and staying there for most of the night.

She knew the story she was supposed to tell: When she was ten, she was biking home from the summer rec program (swimming lessons followed by archery at Spring Creek Park, where she'd line up with the other kids in their shorts and red shirts, holding bows all in a line, squaring off at hay bales with targets spray-painted on their wide sides). She was sweaty, her shirt sticking to her, pumping hard on her bike across the pebbled oil and asphalt road when she saw the roadkill ground squirrel. On the shoulder were two babies, squeaking and shivering. She loaded them into her backpack and pedaled home. She nursed them. She took them to an animal sanctuary. She knew then she wanted to be a vet.

What really happened is that she didn't know what to do. Her cousin Jodi came over and together they the mixed powdered milk with water; very little powder and mostly water. Jodi said the squirrels couldn't handle lactose. Jodi said it should be a very thin liquid. They made nipples with bits of rags, feeding the squalling things. They made a cardboard box with more rags and a heat lamp, but by that evening the smaller one was dead. They called the local animal sanctuary and Sarah's dad drove them out. Later Sarah couldn't bring herself to call and find out if the other one had lived. She looked them up later at the library and found out they were *thirteen-lined ground squirrels*. Somehow reading about their habits and hibernation needs was a substitute for their actual care.

What really happened is that even though Jodi was right, Sarah didn't believe her. Jodi, older and wiser in most ways, had told her to dilute the milk, but Sarah had gone back and added powdered milk, sure that more was better.

What really happened is that Sarah had killed those ground squirrels twice over. Once when she brought them home – she should have just left them. Something would have found them and finished them off; they were making so much noise, some predatory bird, or a cat from the farm across the road, would have been quick and merciful and spared them the hours of suffering Sarah had caused them. She'd prolonged their wobbling, fevered lives, feeding them thickened gruel they couldn't process, taking the live one to the animal sanctuary where it surely died.

She could never do what was needed, what was necessary, always frozen in indecision. The bat with the torn webbing she couldn't finish off. She tried to quiet its squalling, caught in daylight, unable to fly, but couldn't even hit it hard enough with a hammer. In the end, she wrapped it in a dishtowel and hid it under the deck and walked away. There was the deer she hit and drove away from, left shivering in the ditch. (Her older brother kept a gun in the glove box for situations just like that, he'd told her. One of the few times he'd bothered to talk to her, to tell her anything: *Better to put them out of their misery.)*

She always just ran away. She volunteered at a nursing home in high school and, as she was pushing someone's grandmother in her wheelchair, the woman started to fall and again she froze, didn't reach out to stop her, didn't call for help. In the weeks afterward, every time the woman's family came to visit, or she had to help feed her, she had to look at her bruises while her stomach roiled with shame.

But somehow after the ground squirrels, her parents started talking about how she loved animals, how good she was at caring for them. Once, just to get them to stop talking, Sarah said something about being a vet when she grew up. It wasn't a terrible idea. She did prefer to pet the dogs whenever they went anywhere, but that was mostly so she wouldn't have to talk to the people, wouldn't have to try to make friends with other people's kids. Somehow this one thing she said had become a story, a narrative fully-fleshed, so by the time she met with a guidance counselor her sophomore year of high school, the future was formed. Sarah knew exactly what to say whenever some adult asked her, *What do you want to be when you grow up?* all well-meaning and making too much eye contact. And she knew her answer was the right answer, a good answer. She could see it in the way they smiled and relaxed. It wasn't too ambitious.

Or it didn't seem that way. But then when she got to college even that easy answer seemed too much for her. The people here asked follow-up questions. Her advisor asked what *kind* of veterinarian she wanted to be. Her roommate had grown up around horses and had started talking to her about equine care and therapy. Her only experience with animals was with a couple of yellow labs and those ground squirrels. She'd hoped that when classes started it would get better. School was the place where she'd always excelled, but here too Sarah realized she'd made the wrong choice.

In her first-year studies seminar, the professor announced on the first day that there would be no lecture, only discussion – participation would be fifty percent of the grade. In her philosophy course, the professor did 'fishbowl' exercises. She would arrange five chairs in the middle of the classroom with the rest of the class sitting in a larger circle around the interior circle. The students in the small circle were in the 'fishbowl' and were to have the primary discussion. No matter how many times Sarah re-read the day's reading, writing questions and comments in the margins, she'd freeze when it was her turn in the fishbowl. She'd try, she really would, but she'd become bright red, tongue-tied, and unable to contribute. Her time in the fishbowl felt like an eternity. Other students were supposed to tap a fishbowl student (when he or she wasn't talking) to switch places, but the other students didn't know what to do with Sarah, either. Since she hadn't spoken, she had to stay. Her professor would take pity on her. After her second try, her professor asked her to stay after class, and suggested she come to office hours.

Even this was terrible. Her nice professor trying to draw her out, asking if she was OK; sitting across from her at that big desk, looking right at her, commenting on her strong, written work, but asking how she could help her feel more comfortable talking in class. It was all too much – too much eye-contact, too much intrusion, too much gentle-not-gentle handholding, too much to ask of her. Her professor told her she could participate by email and by visiting during office hours to *demonstrate her engagement* with the upcoming group project, as if this wasn't just the fishbowl all over again.

After her midterm grades started to drop and the college's behavioral intervention team got involved, referring her to the campus counselor, Sarah started to harden to all this 'caring,' wondering why no one would just leave her alone. She became immune to her RA's knock, her roommate's wide-eyed questions, the ever-increasing calls from her mother.

Over holiday break, she went to her family doctor who prescribed Lexapro, recommended counseling, and talked about some strategies to deal with her social anxiety. Sarah and her mother looked into the school's resources and made an appointment with student support services for January at the start of the semester.

Sarah signed up for English composition, introduction to psychology, a biology lecture and lab; math, and life drawing. She started to gain back some of the weight she'd lost during her first semester, when she'd taken to hiding in her room instead of risking the chaos of the cafeteria. She made it until early April, after mid-terms and her second bio exam. She made it through the second life drawing class with a male model when her well-developed habit of using the corners of her eyes became a real asset. She made it through her paper about horror movies as cultural artifacts in English (her paper was entitled "Social Anxiety and Slasher Movies"). In the end, it was coming home from the library early to find her dorm room door ajar, hearing her roommate talking about her to girls across the hall, calling her "weird"; talking about how she never made eye contact, suggesting that Sarah was "in love with her," and that was why she always changed in the bathroom. When her roommate left to go visit her boyfriend for the night on the third floor, Sarah packed her things, loaded the car and drove home. And she'd been home ever since. This home that was home for now; her mother and stepfather's house where they still called her room "the guest room."

Carla

Lucy had enjoyed the day, too, but didn't want to let on, not to Dr. Larsen. She was telling Carla about it over dinner before going over the schedule for next week. The contractor was coming out on Monday to go over plans for the pool. They were hoping to start work next spring as soon as the ground thawed. To do that, they'd want to get the plans approved, connect the architect and the contractor, and get any necessary permits. They were well aware that the contractor thought they were nuts. Who puts an in-ground pool inside, in this climate, attached to a modest ranch house? They were hoping to discuss their rationale with him on Monday, and that when he saw all the plans, including the handicapped-accessible bathroom, he'd understand they weren't just a couple of eccentric ladies, but rather that this was related to health concerns. In the end, it wouldn't be a problem once the deposit check cleared.

Lucy was going over to Tracy's again on Wednesday afternoon to work on leash training, and help with some boundary work with Stella. After today's events at the vet office, she was hoping that Tracy wouldn't be too freaked out; she figured she'd call her tomorrow to check in.

Lucy also wanted to ask Carla about another project: Sarah. She'd been watching the young vet tech, and thinking that maybe she could benefit from a little confidence-building herself. With the number of new clients Lucy had taken on who wanted in-home work with their dogs, and Carla's mobility issues getting worse, they could use a little extra help caring for their own animals. Lucy was hoping Carla would be open to Sarah coming out and helping with the afternoon chores.

The new in-home work was interesting. Since Lucy had helped the town library with their Dog Days programming, pairing the summer reading program attendees with rescue dogs and meeting a bunch of the wealthy, volunteer ladies who summer on the big lake, everybody wanted some extra training and manners work – but only on their time and at their homes.

At first she'd demurred, uncertain how this would work. But pretty soon Lucy had realized she could charge higher rates for the convenience of house calls, and the dogs were mostly pampered, city pets who were out of their element when left to their own devices over the summer, with broad lawns to run and their only exercise unsupervised swimming. The extra money was useful, and the dogs and owners were mostly nice, although it took a while to get used to calling them 'pet parents' and the dogs 'companion animals,' or whatever that particular rich person insisted on. Lucy kept a detailed page for each household and reviewed it before each visit: the giant schnauzers who were named after German generals (she was a little worried about that household's politics, had blanched when they introduced her to Rommel); the rescue dogs named Baby and Honey (who were cooked full, human-quality meals every day); the pack of bearded collies whose grooming alone must have taken hours. But Lucy's training techniques seemed to improve the dogs' lives, as well as their people's, so word-of-mouth had spread like wildfire and she was booked weeks in advance.

After dinner, while Lucy was loading the dishwasher and Carla was still sitting at the table, their cocker spaniel mix, Jake, laying at her feet, Carla brought up her own agenda item.

"Luce, do you remember when I asked you to marry me?"

Lucy was wringing out the dishrag, stuffing the last bits of romaine down the garbage disposal. It was a moment almost as romantic as when Carla had first proposed.

"Yup," Lucy turned and smiled at her.

A couple of weeks ago, the Supreme Court had officially ruled that Lucy and Carla, along with every couple – gay or straight – had a fundamental right to marry. They'd both been watching TV when it was announced, and let out a whoop. The dogs came running, and their old cat startled where it slept most of the day on the back of the couch. They were hopeful, but cautiously so; it had looked good before. Last summer, the state's ban on gay marriage had been found unconstitutional, but the governor appealed the decision. Then that October, the state's appellate court refused to hear the appeal. Some counties granted marriage licenses, some didn't. At the time, Lucy had asked Carla what all that meant; Carla said she thought they should wait for the Supreme Court. And now that decision had gone their way, but some clerks and judges were saying they wouldn't honor the Court's decision, so they thought maybe they should wait a little longer, to see how everything shook out. There were some clerks who refused to grant any marriage licenses, so as not to grant them to gay couples. There were a few so-called 'defense of religious freedom' bills proposed, and it was unclear what effect they'd have, whether they'd pass constitutional tests.

Lucy and Carla had already waited so long. When Carla had first said they should wait for the Supreme Court last summer, Lucy had been sitting on the edge of the couch cushions, her head cocked toward the TV, watching the talking heads debate the patchwork of laws across the country and what they meant. Carla was leaning heavily on her crutches, standing in the archway between the living room and the kitchen.

"I've been thinking," Carla said, pausing to scratch Jake's ears, "if you still want to marry me, we could do that next summer."

"Why next summer?"

"Put the pool in and have a luau," Carla said, winking.

"A luau?"

"And I was thinking we could do it on July second."

Carla continued tenderly working a matted patch of fur while the dog whined ever so slightly. Carla had always had gentle hands, hands that knew what to do. When Carla's hands palmed Lucy's hips, her ball and socket joints hummed.

"What's July second?"

"That was my mother's birthday."

Growing up, Carla remembered never having enough space. Their trailer was small – a long hallway, two bedrooms, the tiny bathroom, a combo kitchen/dining/living room. She shared a room with her sister until her sister left. Carla mostly remembered trying to make herself as small as possible, to shrink into corners whenever she could find a corner. Between her father's anger, usually fueled by too many drinks, and her mother's pain, there never seemed to be much space for whatever Carla was feeling anyway. Peggy took the opposite approach. As she became a teenager, she grew tall and taller, loud and louder, and she fought with her parents for every square inch she could. When Peggy still lived with them, the best Carla could do was avoid one fight or another.

At first, Carla didn't understand how what Peggy did was so wrong. She didn't get bad grades or mouth off in school; she brought home her pay from whatever part-time job she worked after school or during the summer, but it was something about how she looked directly at their father, held her head too high, disagreed on even the little things that started every fight. If he wanted French fries for dinner, then she'd want tater tots. If he wanted tater tots, she'd start making French fries. It never really seemed to mean anything, other than that was what she wanted. Wanted things, her own things, things that were different than what he thought she should want.

Carla and Peggy's mother knew only ever to agree with anything their father said, even if it was clearly not the right thing. When the girls were too little to understand why their mother did this, they'd be puzzled. Like when he'd say, "I don't know why I have to come home to no dinner on the table," and dinner had been there, waiting, but he'd been half-drunk already and had stumbled past it. Their mother never pointed out the waiting plate, wrapped in plastic, the carefully portioned parts of dinner she'd made and set aside when it was clear he wasn't going to be home when he said he was. When Carla and Peggy were little, they didn't understand that this was what their mother meant when she said they'd have to settle down and learn how to be wives.

But as Peggy got older, she got louder and louder. She experimented with hair dye from the drug store, finally settling on a shade of red that her mother said might as well be called 'Harlot.' (Carla didn't know what this meant until she looked it up in the dictionary.) Peggy brought home her paychecks dutifully, gloated over her grades, but refused to pretend that her father was a good father, that he was right, that he wasn't a drunk. As Peggy got more and more willful, their father turned from yelling to the belt, and their mother turned an even more inward quiet, reading the Bible in the front room of the trailer, flinching ever so slightly at the sound of the leather hitting skin in the back bedroom, at the not-sound of Peggy refusing to cry out.

Carla never got the belt. She learned her lessons vicariously through Peggy. Peggy who refused to wear long sleeves to cover any bruises, who refused to stay home from school even when her mother asked her to, her mother's voice quavering, her mother's arms open to hug her, and Peggy walking right past those arms to go out the trailer's flimsy door and catch a ride to school, almost eager to show off the damage done by her father's anger and her mother's complacence. As soon as Peggy could, she got the hell out of that trailer. And Carla was stuck – until she met Sammy.

Sammy was a quiet kid, too – the son of the preacher at her mother's new church. This new church was non-denominational, a place where everyone called each other 'brother' or 'sister,' where people spoke in strange, gurgling sounds, and vacation Bible school had guitar lessons and overnight lock-ins. At one of these lock-ins, where Carla went just to get away from her parents and the trailer for a blessed night, she met Sammy sitting off by himself, avoiding the fervent sing-along happening in the fellowship hall. If she'd known he was the preacher's son, she probably wouldn't have talked to him, but he seemed as uncomfortable as she was. He was pale and sweaty, in clothes that didn't quite fit, and the other kids avoided him just like they avoided Carla.

Carla's mother had started coming to this church soon after the hair-dye incident, when she became convinced that Peggy was *Going down the wrong road.* She'd sit for hours at the eat-in table in the kitchen, the only halo the dim light caught in her own frazzled hair. Her Bible reading became protracted and intense right around then, but it wasn't clear if that was because she was worried about her older daughter's waywardness, or because her husband had upped his punishment strategy, switched from using the end tip of the belt to the buckle, behind the closed door at the end of the hallway. Either way, she found a new church that forbid drinking, insisted on below-the-knee skirts, and began taking her younger daughter with her every Sunday.

Carla and Sammy met the summer before they both began high school and they became each other's only friends for the next two years. Quiet, shambling Carla who rarely spoke above a whisper at school, who never spoke at home, only nodding, her eyes averted; and Sammy, pale and sweaty, even in winter; hair so black it was blue, the only child of the preacher from the weird church that was rumored to have tongue-speakers and snake-handlers. No other kids had any interest in them, so they pretended to have no interest in any other kids. They both did all right in school, not excelling because that might draw attention, but not doing poorly, either. They endured their parents' mostly benign interest in their friendship, not understanding until too late that maybe everyone else was getting their hopes up. Carla's mother thought that maybe if her youngest daughter married a preacher's son it would make up for her oldest daughter being a 'Whore of Babylon.' (It was rumored that since Peggy had moved out, she was living with a man, although she was still attending high school and would graduate.) Sammy's parents thought Carla would make an ideal preacher's wife: quiet and dutiful, not good-looking, not asking for, or wanting too much.

Over the next two years the parents watched approvingly as the two shy teenagers seemed to seek each other out. Carla would help make coffee before services and stay after to hand out cookies and muffins, clean the church kitchen. Sammy would stay after as well, then walk Carla home – or close to home. Carla wouldn't let him come to the door of the trailer, or even turn down the little half street in their subdivision within the trailer park. And Carla and Sammy, observing their parents and their desires, nursed rich and perverse desires of their own, which they occasionally shared, testing how they sounded out loud, speaking them only to each other.

They both hated their parents, they told each other. On the walks home, although it may have looked like a scene from *The Andy Griffith Show*, they were spilling secrets of their parents' secret vices and weaknesses. Sammy knew about Carla's father's drinking and cruelty; the way her mother believed that if she read the Bible enough she was somehow exonerated from protecting Peggy from the smile she'd surely seen on her own husband's face as he was meting out punishment, the leather singing as it arced through the air. Sammy told her about his father's collection of pornography, his mother's boyfriends, the way they lied all day, every day to everyone at the church, to him, to each other. On these walks, and on the summer afternoons they'd steal away, they'd make up terrible punishments for their terrible parents, imagining them dying in accidents that weren't accidents, imagining a truly just God revealing them for the hypocrites they were, freeing Sammy and Carla from the roles they had to play. Mostly they fantasized about escape.

It was during one of these conversations about a "just" God when Sammy told Carla that he didn't believe in God. Carla gasped. Even after the play-by-play fairy tales where their parents were crushed to death, or stabbed by travelling killers, this seemed a truly evil thing to say. Sammy's eyes were welling up and he took Carla's hands and told her he'd never told anyone this before, but he just felt so close to her.

"I just don't believe in God," he said again, "and someday I'm going to tell my father that."

Carla thought Sammy was the bravest person she knew, next to Peggy. But his was a different kind. She wished someday she could be brave enough to be who she was, to say what she was thinking, to someday just stop pretending all the time. But as she was thinking this, Sammy leaned over and kissed her. His breath smelled like the ketchup from the hot dogs they'd eaten earlier at the Perry Patch, a patio restaurant that was only open in the summer. Their parents were so happy with the time they spent together that they often gave them a dollar or two, if they had plans. If they pooled their money, they could afford two hotdogs, and a banana split to share. Carla always let Sammy have the cherry and most of the whip cream.

She was so startled by the kiss, even more so than by what he'd just told her about God, that she blurted out "No!" and pulled back, losing her balance on the log they were sitting on (at the edge of the woods behind the high school), and she landed flat on her back. Now the back of her skirt and shirt would be dirty and someone – her mother probably – would be suspicious, thinking something else had happened. They were both going to be juniors this year, and her mother had been asking if she and Sammy were "going steady," not even bothering to be coy about her questions or her hints. She'd probably be pleased to see the stains on her clothes, thinking it was proper and right that they'd moved on to this next stage.

"Sorry," Sammy said. "I didn't mean to surprise you."

"No," Carla said again, but softer this time, "it's just..." She stood up, brushing the back of her clothes. "I didn't... I mean..." She looked at Sammy and didn't know what to say. Their mocking of their parents had always included this, the way their parents imagined something romantic between them. She always thought that she and Sammy agreed on this as well – they were friends, really good friends.

Sammy took her hand, now that she was upright and looking at him, and then he moved in for another kiss. "No!" she said again and, this time, pushed him away.

"What Carla?" he said, trying to keep his voice even, but maybe a little hurt, maybe a little angry. "I thought you liked me?"

"I do, Sammy. I love you, you're my best friend, but I didn't, I didn't know you liked me like that…" She stopped talking, she didn't really know how or what to say.

"I didn't really know either until just now, telling you how I really felt. I've never told anyone that before – I just felt so close to you."

"Oh," Carla said.

They didn't see each other until the following Sunday, and by then Carla had thought long and hard about her best friend and what he had confided in her, how he had trusted her, and what that meant. She wanted to let him know how much she cared about him and to repay his trust. And she wanted him to know that the reason she didn't kiss him back had nothing to do with him – if she liked boys, she would have liked him; he was so kind, and funny, and smart. But she didn't like boys and she never had. She didn't plan on ever liking boys, or dating, or getting married, not like that. She hoped he would understand and that they could go back to being friends the way they were. His friendship meant so much to her.

They went for a walk after the service and talked, and for once Carla felt brave and she said everything she meant to say to Sammy, holding his hand just like he had when he'd told her what he really thought about God. And then they went back to the church to help with coffee and fellowship. Carla helped the ladies in the kitchen, but didn't see much of Sammy and she walked herself home. As she turned onto the half street, she could see boxes outside of their trailer, her mother bent over. She walked up to the narrow strip of burnt summer grass and dirt they called the front lawn, just as her mother went back in the trailer and shut the door. Carla reached for the handle and heard the click as it locked from inside, heard her mother say "Abomination." Her voice hissed like a slim welt of leather in the air.

Carla didn't know what to do, so she sat on the metal grate step, and waited. She waited for the door to open, for her mother to say something else, to come back outside, to hear her father's TV waft through an open window, but those too were shut tight. Clouds gathered and it looked like rain. She was still wearing her church dress, a pale yellow below-the-knee with sleeves and a smocked front, a pattern of small cornflowers smattered all over. It started to sprinkle, then rain, and still she sat on the metal step, her hair wet and matted down her back, and shivered. The rain was soaking the cardboard boxes where her clothes and books waited, warping, ruining. Headlights approached and stopped. It was Peggy.

"Dad called," she said. "Get in."

A rangy boy got out of the driver's side and started to load her three boxes into the trunk. "This is Lorne," Peggy said, giving her meaningful eyes.

Carla slowly stood up and walked toward her big sister. Peggy's hair was an even brighter shade of red, piled up high on top of her head, her eyes rimmed in black eye shadow. Carla hadn't seen her since school in the spring, when she'd graduated. Peggy gathered her in her arms, impossibly long and thin.

"It'll be OK, little sister. We'll talk about it later – not in front of Lorne though, OK?"

Sarah's first few days helping with the animals did not go well. Lucy had taken two whole afternoons to do the chores with her, introducing her to the animals, and showing her the routines, before giving her the freedom to find her own rhythm. Carla had worried right away, had known the horses would spook her, but since her rheumatoid arthritis was in flare right then, she knew she'd be of little help.

The first day of Sarah doing the chores solo, it seemed she knocked on the door every fifteen minutes, double-checking some instruction or another: Which horse was likely to kick? Which switch turned off the electric fence? Was it the second or third bin that held the feed for the llama-alpaca mixes? The first few times Sarah knocked Carla didn't even hear it, the rapping was so quiet. The second day of Sarah doing the chores solo, Carla was ready, had gotten a book, and set herself up on the back deck within yelling distance of the barn, but this only seemed to increase Sarah's dependence on her, her unwillingness to complete any task without a quick check-in. Each night when Carla reported the drawn-out routine to Lucy, how the short schedule had dragged out to hours (sighing with impatience), her beloved had put her hand gingerly on Carla's forearm, careful not to trigger any more pain and asked her to wait out the young woman, reminded her how useless she'd been when Carla had first met her.

On the third day of Sarah's solo chores, the Friday of the third week of July, things improved. Carla got through a whole chapter of her book with

Sarah only interrupting her once, sheepishly, to ask if there was a way to lure Thelma, the watch donkey, back into the enclosure. Carla looked up to see their wayward donkey locking eyes with Goose, the good-for-nothing border collie, over the chain link fence between their back yard and the dirt road that ended in their driveway. In some ways, Goose and Thelma were natural enemies and natural allies, or should have been. Goose should have been working for some farmer, helping him herd sheep, but the dog refused to herd. Thelma should have been protecting the flock from wolves, but the damn donkey was too shy of people to be much good, so it would charge anything dog-like but run away from its owners. For the most part, Thelma just hung out with the other animals, but if someone – in this case Sarah – forgot to close the gate, the donkey either took to the hills, or went looking for trouble; trouble was ginning up a fight with Goose. At this point, Carla and Lucy were blissfully sheep-free.

"Uh oh," Lucy's voice rang out as she came around the front of the house, holding two boxes of pizza and a six pack, "looks like Thelma got out." Sarah turned red-faced to Lucy, as she started to inch toward the donkey.

"Stay right there, Sarah. If you spook her, it'll take all night to catch her."

Luckily, Thelma's kryptonite was bananas. Lucy grabbed a few from the house, and laid a banana trail heading back to the barn. Once the donkey was in, they shut the gate. Before returning to the deck for dinner, Lucy and Sarah spent a few minutes petting and playing with the kittens who were quickly becoming asshole, adolescent cats and efficient mousers. At first, Sarah had declined to stay for dinner, but Lucy asked again – pointed out that she'd gotten two pizzas, and that if Sarah didn't stay, she'd have to drink a beer all by herself. So Sarah called home and told her mother to eat without her. Between the escaped donkey, the banana trick, the fact that Lucy was a vegetarian and Carla a recovering alcoholic, Sarah thought she'd had an eventful evening already, full of surprises. But then, just after passing around the plates and cloth napkins, Lucy leaned over and kissed Carla full on the mouth.

While Sarah was still quiet, Lucy filled the space. Her appointment with the Nazi Schnauzers had been cancelled, so she'd stopped to check on Tracy and Stella, see how it was going. Tracy'd been working on the leash training with Smoke and Red, using a head collar, and they'd both stopped pulling so much on the walks, and walking Stella alone, she'd even made some new friends.

"Some older guy who walks his dog on the trestle trail north of town," Lucy said between bites of veggie pizza. "Guess he has a labradoodle and his dog and Stella are buddies now."

"So Stella didn't try to corner him up against a tree?" Carla asked laughing. Sarah looked up, smiling. "Oh, I forgot – you were there."

"You heard about that?" Sarah was eating her slice of sausage carefully, just barely smiling.

"Sure," Carla answered. "Stuck at home here I get regaled with the fascinating stories of The Prospect Street Vet Clinic." Lucy threw her balled-up napkin at her. "No, seriously, that one was actually pretty funny."

"It *was* funny," Lucy said, fake-pleading.

"I know, that's what I said," Carla smiled, winked at Sarah.

"I feel kind of bad for laughing," Sarah said, but she wasn't even laughing, not really.

He shouldn't have smacked her on the ass like that," Lucy said. "Some girls don't like that."

"Nope, some don't," Carla laughed again.

Sarah had never really spent any time with lesbians, although she knew a lot people thought she was one, and not just her college roommate. Spending time out at the farm would probably only increase other people's suspicions, especially her mother's, once she found out about Lucy and Carla. Partly, it was that Sarah had never had a boyfriend, had never even been out on a date. Sarah didn't think she was a lesbian though, because as much as she had no interest in boys in high school or college, or even now, she didn't have any interest in girls, either. She always thought that maybe it was a part of her anxiety, this lack of interest. Even when she was younger, and the few friends she had started talking about boys or getting crushes on TV actors and boy bands, she'd mostly had to fake it to fit in, practicing saying *Cuuuute!* with just the right amount of upward lilt in her voice.

After she dropped out of college, her first counselor had reminded her of her philosophy professor. She was in her mid-forties, wore wrap dresses, and had soft grey eyes. She had a throaty laugh. She was the kind of woman that other people would describe as "sexy"; Sarah knew this, but she didn't get it. The counselor asked Sarah if she masturbated. Sarah didn't even know how to answer, how to talk about something like that. Talking about dating and coming up with excuses was one thing (her school work, being too tired, her social anxiety) – all those seemed to work with most people. But this woman seemed to be asking something else – not about who Sarah liked, but about her own body's pleasure. It might have been the first time Sarah stood up for herself. She told her counselor she didn't want to talk about it. The truth was Sarah's body didn't seem to work like that, it didn't seem to want and respond the way other people's bodies did. But she always thought this was just one more thing wrong with her, something else that was broken about her. Being around Lucy and Carla made her think that maybe there were other ways to be than the few ways she thought people had to be.

After dinner Lucy and Sarah cleaned up, and walked back out to the barn, talked about the week and how it was going. Sarah started apologizing for how slow she was, how long it took her to catch on, about letting Thelma out. Lucy walked around the barn with her one more time, checking on the animals, mentioning out loud how they already seemed comfortable with her, thanking her for straightening out the tools in the corner, asking if she wanted to keep coming out afternoons. Lucy mentioned that there were a lot of people who didn't seem to know that she and Carla were together, glossing over Sarah's surprise earlier, excusing her moment of discomfort. She mentioned a few of Carla's health problems and that when she had a flare, she just couldn't do much physical activity at all, and even on good days, hauling feed and looking after the horses was too much for her; a walk back and forth from the barn was rough on her joints. Sarah could really help them out if she was up for it. They negotiated a weekly wage. Near the end of the conversation, Lucy casually dropped into the conversation that she didn't want to take Sarah away from her family if she'd rather be at home, but if she'd like a little excuse to not be, they could oblige. Sarah looked out of the corner of her eyes and almost smiled.

Kindness

It was funny to Sarah how the people most people overlooked could sometimes be the most helpful, the most kind. She'd probably had half a dozen therapists who'd tried to help her figure out what she was so afraid of, why she couldn't seem to interact like normal people, what it was that made small, everyday interaction so fraught for her. She'd had so many people in her life try to help her – her mother and stepfather, certainly, and that philosophy professor in college – but none of them did help her, or so it seemed. And then there'd be the oddballs, people like Dr. Schulz the veterinarian. When he'd hired Donna to be the part-time receptionist, most of the regular customers were shocked. They'd come in for their appointments and startle and swallow a little before they could reply to her perfectly pleasant, "How may I help you?" In this small town the news that Donna was working at the vet clinic spread like wildfire, but Dr. Schulz kept her right there at the front desk, as visible as could be until everyone calmed down. He never said anything to anyone. Maybe he never even said anything to Donna either, but Sarah knew what Dr. Schulz was doing.

Donna used to work for one of the big real estate firms until she was convicted of embezzling funds. She spent a few years in prison. No one would know it to look at her; she looked like anyone's mother or aunt, but she had a criminal record, and a reputation. While she was in prison, her husband left her and they divorced quietly, shortly before she got out. She never explained what happened, and never had since she'd been out. For the amount of money she'd taken, people thought that maybe she'd bought a boat or a lake cabin, or she had some secret gambling problem. But she just kept wearing her grandma cardigans with cats and owls on them, going to Shear Design for her haircuts, driving her Ford Taurus station wagon, bringing her beef and noodle hot dish to every potluck. She never went to trial, just pled guilty. So no one ever knew what happened.

But there were theories – or those people who knew her son had theories. Her son had a bad cocaine habit and had taken to dealing. If she'd really taken the money, he must have needed it, and needed it badly. But Donna wasn't talking. If she'd thought it would save him, get him out of whatever trouble he was in, turn him around, or help him get clean, that hadn't worked either. So after she'd paid her debt to society and Dr. Schulz had hired her, Donna answered phones and made appointments at the vet clinic, smiling at anyone who walked through the door. Anyone who wanted to could keep imagining her secret life as she drove her station wagon home to her empty house, waiting to hear from her only child who rarely called.

When Sarah decided to go back to school for the vet tech program, she knew she'd need some help, so she started a cognitive-behavioral therapy program at a clinic in Appleton. She had a therapist and group. The program was designed to teach her small behaviors she could learn and practice on her own, to help her navigate the everyday moments, and build to the kind of interactions she'd need to be successful in school. She did OK, but what she remembered was meeting Aaron.

They weren't in the same group (he was with the depressed people), but as she was waiting between her individual appointment and the group session, he'd be leaving his group session and waiting for his individual appointment. She doesn't remember how they started talking or why. Talking to strangers, to strange men, wasn't something Sarah did. Aaron was a little older than her and overweight. He dressed mostly in grey and black, in shapeless t-shirts and Dickies work pants, and his skin was pale and scaly. Because she knew how painful it was when people stared, she tried not to stare. The first time he talked to her, she remembered that he sat next to her at a table, not across from her, and that he left a chair between them. Maybe he knew she was one of the social anxiety people, maybe he had some of that of his own, but she was able to talk to him a little, looking out of the corner of her eyes, and she didn't feel pressured, or stared at, or like she was in a fishbowl.

After that, they'd see each other on Thursdays, when their paths would cross, and usually he'd have something for her, or something for them to share. It was always a weird thing – nothing big or special, but it usually made her laugh. Except that she didn't laugh, not out loud, but she'd smile a little, and look at him sideways, and he'd laugh his kind of laugh that was like a deep burble from the fat of his belly. The first time he brought something for her it was a can of Orange Crush, a bag of Andy Capp's Hot Fries, and a clementine. He had his own set. He pushed the small pile toward her at the table, still sitting parallel, a chair away, and said, "Lunch."

"What?" Sarah asked, mostly looking down.

"Lunch," he repeated. "Orange."

Another day he brought a bag of finger traps – the kind they have at arcades for cheap prizes. Four tickets for a finger trap; a finger in each side and the harder it's pulled, the harder it holds, made of woven raffia and painted in fluorescent stripes. After a few tugs, they unraveled and fell apart. She and Aaron played around with the finger traps for an hour, destroying the whole bag. The gifts were odd; he was odd. But he was the first person she'd talked to and made friends with on her own. Sitting next to him, his companionable strangeness, made her feel good, whole. But one Thursday he wasn't there and then he wasn't there again. She enrolled in the local tech school and completed her program in one and a half years. She never saw Aaron again.

Meetings

It was happening again – that feeling Tracy got in her chest, that unreasonable anticipation; her heart beating fast, her breath coming quickly, almost like sex. But all she was doing was pulling the creeping charlie that had grown in under the ferns in the late July heat, after a few drenching rains. It was so satisfying, the shallow roots, the long tendrils. If she pulled the right vine, the whole clump would come out, a long tangle of leaves and stems and the strange orb-like fruits along with it, with their peculiar smell, their tang. She straightened up for a moment and could hear Stella's chuff. She looked up to see a woman who looked like her mother stop at the intersection of sidewalk and the walk to her front porch.

"Mom?" she asked, pushing her bangs out of her eyes, brushing the dirt off her knees. "Hi."

"Tracy... hello. I was just on my way to the library and," she stopped and looked up to the porch, where Stella's boxy head was resting on the gate blocking off the brick porch, "and that looks like one of the dogs your father mentioned," she finished, nodding toward the porch.

"That's Stella," Tracy threw a clump of the creeping charlie into the fern fronds and joined her mother. "Um, can I invite you in?"

"I'd like that." Her mother smiled.

Tracy's mother had only been to her house maybe once or twice, always to drop something off. Usually, Tracy visited her parent's house, or they communicated by telephone; if necessary, they'd meet for dinner – on Mother's Day, or a birthday. Since Tracy and her father had returned from Idaho, they'd all been together once, and Tracy and her mother had spoken for maybe ten minutes. Every time Aaron's name came up, her mother's eyes filled with tears and neither Tracy or her father knew what to do, so they wandered off, leaving her to herself.

Tracy put all three dogs in the backyard and made a pot of coffee. She and her mother sat at the kitchen table, drinking out of the big, hand-made mugs Tracy'd bought from a local potter (the kind that had to be handwashed, that couldn't be put into the microwave or the dishwasher). Her mother looked "smart" (that was the word she would have used). Her blondish hair was streaked with grey, in a way that looked like highlights, caught back behind her ears. She was wearing a fitted button-down shirt over a linen skirt and wedge sandals. She had a fresh manicure and pedicure, and she seemed quite a bit *lighter* than the last time they'd been together. After a couple minutes of sipping and the obligatory small talk, Tracy finally asked.

"Well, I've started volunteering at the library..." her mother burst out, a little breathless. "We have this program, called *Dog Days* where we work with the local animal shelter, with their rescue dogs, and with some of the elementary school kids. This wonderful woman Lucy..."

"Lucy Stillwater?"

"Yes! Do you know Lucy?"

"She's helping me with the dogs. Go on, Mom."

"Well, there's this idea that with children who have reading difficulties that dogs can help, that they're non-judgmental, they just listen. So we pair dogs with children, all supervised, of course, and it helps the dogs too," she took a quick sip of coffee, "and already we've had such success!"

Tracy hadn't seen her mother this *animated* in quite a while, probably since before Aaron had started to withdraw, when it was clear that he was sick and that it wasn't something he was just going to snap out of. As those months turned into years, her mother had started to insulate herself, to make smaller and smaller movements, as if she were wrapped in a layer of thick cotton batting; as if any quickness, or too much excitement, too much energy, could shatter some careful balance she'd worked hard to achieve. But here she was talking about individual kids and specific dogs. She told Tracy how some families had fostered a dog and then adopted it. Her mother seemed to be partial to a setter mix named Angel.

At the third mention of that dog, Tracy interrupted to ask, "Are you going to adopt a dog?"

"Oh no," she said quickly, "can you imagine? Your father was already worried when I said I was coming over here. He gave me quite an earful about your dogs."

Those dogs seemed unconcerned about Tracy's guest. From their vantage point in the kitchen, mother and daughter could see Smoke rolling and rubbing herself on the lawn, belly up and grunting. Red was sniffing the periphery of the fence, head down, intent, following Stella's lead. Since Stella's rabbits had grown and hopped away, she seemed to spend a lot of time sniffing the perimeter, mostly around the gate. When she had a really good scent, as she seemed to now, she went stock-still, her tail straight out, the bristles on her withers up.

"Your old friend stopped over the other day," her mother said. "He has a new business. Landscaping, mowing, that sort of thing."

"He's not my friend, Mom."

"Tracy, can I ask – whatever happened there?"

"He cheated on me, Mom."

"Oh, well, good for you," she set her cup down firmly. "If they do that once and get away with it, they'll just keep doing it."

After her mother left, Tracy let the dogs back in. They made a straight path from the back door to the living room, avoiding the kitchen. This was a new routine. Lucy had suggested Tracy designate a few dog-free areas of the house, including the kitchen. Tracy had only had to reinforce the boundary a few times before Stella learned it and, as always, the two pits followed her lead, observing an invisible line at the doorframe. If Tracy was cooking bacon or something else delectable, they'd lie down in order: Stella first, then Smoke, then Red, but never crossing that invisible line. Tracy had also made the guest room off-limits (useful for the few times Cal had spent the night) and the bathroom (especially after Stella had surprised him during one late-night trip when he hadn't bothered to switch on the light).

Lucy had also taught Tracy the "Leave it!" command, which had proven to be the most useful and, most used, directive she gave the dogs. It worked with dropped food, the baby rabbits, new people, and Cal. The next time her mother visited, after her library shift the next week, she'd use the command to limit the amount of shed fur and drool the dogs would deposit on her mother's clothes. Despite her mother's request, Tracy had suggested they wait until she was done at the library to meet the dogs. Although her mother's style was simple, her clothes were nice, and Tracy didn't want her to show up with the other summer ladies wearing Stella's trademark markings, provided the dog was feeling up for a close sniff.

Overall, most of Lucy's suggestions had worked well with the dogs. Likely Smoke and Red would always be dog-aggressive, and never be the kind of animals that could just run up and meet other dogs. But they were sweet with people and now that they had learned to walk on leashes, Tracy really enjoyed their daily walks. At first, the head collar and the stop and start training had been tiresome, but she'd stuck with it. The dogs learned that any pulling meant Tracy immediately switched direction, even if it meant they'd covered no ground, just reversed course over and over again in front of the house for an hour until they learned not to pull. After about a week of that, they were going around the block, and now they could walk at a good steady pace, with no leash-tangling, unless a squirrel or loose dog set them off.

And walking Stella was a pleasure. They'd taken to the trestle trail to avoid running into people, but discovered several other dog walkers who also liked the solitude of the trail and were up for getting to know a dog like her. The biggest surprise was Jack, who walked his doodle, Willy, there. Jack looked to be in his mid-fifties, and mostly talked about what fish were biting, between pointing out the different kinds of birds and water fowl.

The first time they met, the man had been walking toward them, the blonde dog also off-leash, and Tracy had started to tense up, but Stella stayed right with her and gently made friends with the strange-looking dog. (Jack always cracked jokes about his dog, claiming it didn't look quite right – more poodle than anything else, a strange, matted coat and double-curled tail, and bounced around like it was on springs.) But the dogs were both silent, neither barked, and they both took any chance they could to dip into the water-logged ditches that bordered the trail, or the slough, or the mill-pond that bloomed with lotus and water lily. Jack seemed perfectly content to wait Stella out, and something about his doodle relaxed her, too. Before long, the big tough-looking dog would recognize the pair coming on the trail and would run and butt her head against the man, asking for affection. Otherwise, Stella stayed close off-lead, never more than ten feet ahead of or behind Tracy. It was the closest companionship she'd had since she and Aaron had been little kids.

The biggest thing Lucy helped Tracy figure out was how to create psychological boundaries between her and the dogs. What a strange thing to have to learn, to have to be told, however gently Lucy had tried to nudge her toward it. Tracy was adept at keeping people away, but she needed to be told to carve out and maintain some space for herself with the dogs – especially with Stella. *Don't let the dog lean on her; claim her own space. Don't let the dog crowd her, or push her out of her own bed. Don't let the dog interfere with her own needs and her own desires.*

The first time Cal came over and was going to spend the night, Tracy actually had a hard time shutting the door to the guest room, the room she tried to keep relatively free of fur and dander and allergens, so that she and Cal could take each other's clothes off, and do with each other what they liked. Stella made a sound like keening beyond the door, and for a while it was hard for Tracy to get into it, to let her body respond, even though Cal was right there, rubbing her nipples with his callused fingertips. Eventually she forgot about the dogs, but after, when Cal went to the bathroom, she remembered he called, "Tracy?" his voice a little high-pitched. She found him in the bathroom, naked, still and frozen, Stella in the doorway, staring him down.

"Leave it," she said.

Cal was at Salty's, cooling down with a beer after meeting with some homeowners on the lake who wanted restoration done on their chimney and the stonework on their house. It was a strange house, one of the oldest on the lake. Rumor had it that it had been designed by an acolyte of Frank Lloyd Wright. It did have low-hanging eaves and the esoteric use of stone throughout the house; a big boulder jutted up into the living room. But the claim had never been substantiated and the house was an oddity. The current owners loved it though, and Cal could see why.

The roof needed repair, and there'd need to be some work on the foundation, maybe some drainage tiles installed. The contractor had called Cal to see if he wanted to handle the stonework on the chimney and foundation. He'd have to try to match and source some stone. In addition to repairs, the owners wanted to add some landscaping, and erect some dry-laid stone walls. Cal knew a guy who could help with that (an artisan really) – if he could find the stone. And Cal had been wanting to learn more about working in dry stone.

Luke was going to meet him when he got off work, but in the meantime, Cal had taken a seat at the bar, next to a few other guys who looked like they'd just gotten done with work, too. The late July weather was warmer than usual for a Wisconsin summer and the humidity was high, too. Working near the lake made it worse – all that shimmering blue calling over the expanse of manicured lawns, the boats bobbing at the end of docks; ski boats and pontoons and sailboats, and none of the lake accessible to Cal or any of the other guys who worked for the rich people who owned the green or the boats or thought they owned the shimmering blue. Guys like Cal just got to go to the local bar and cool down with a beer, the sweat drying and sticking their shirts to their skin, the dust of mown grass and blown dirt gritting their hair and beards.

The guy beside Cal had a close-cropped beard too, and sunburned cheeks and the particular green dusting of someone who rode a mower all day. The deposit of grass trimmings and lawn chemicals mixed with sweat identified him as someone who'd probably stared at the blue over the shoulder of someone who was paying him – just like Cal. They were both downing their beers quickly, as if they were water, nodding to the bartender for another. Cal was thinking about Tracy.

Things with Tracy were going pretty well: they'd been out a few times, had had sex a few times, spent the night together a few times. She was funny and smart. Last weekend he'd had dinner at her house, and they'd sat out late in the backyard. The neighbor Deborah had come over, calling him "Sexy Beardy," and getting a little sloppy. But the cicadas had been singing and the dogs were running around and playing – even Stella – and thanks to his allergy medicine and everyone's good mood, he was starting to think that this could be something, this could work. He'd spent the night (in the guest room, what Tracy called the "dog-free" room) and he'd appreciated that she'd thought of this, thought of him, of a way to make him more comfortable.

The sheets and bedding were pale and crisp, old-fashioned with an embroidered hem, and the tall windows were open to the backyard. The evening wind whipped up before a rainstorm, and the cool air rushed in. It had taken Tracy a little while to get warmed up, to start making her noises, to get loud – something that both embarrassed and turned him on. When she got really loud, with the windows still open, he'd laughed and tried to cover her mouth, but she'd wriggled away from him, saying that it was her house, those were her neighbors, that there were a lot worse noises to be concerned about. When she came, her noises were throaty and finally high-pitched. Later, when he was in the bathroom, still thinking about her sitting astride him, legs clenching, with her fingers in his mouth, Stella had surprised him. She'd butted him between his legs with her nose, then stood in the doorway, staring him down.

The next morning he made a frittata (the only thing he knew how to make) in one of her big cast-iron skillets, and they ate on the patio table in the backyard. He'd kept a wary eye on Stella, but she kept her distance, too.

Tracy pointed out the husk of a cicada perched on the back of the chair; it hadn't been there last night. He remembered seeing a cicada molting on a camping trip with his sister and Dad and Mom, shortly before she was diagnosed. It was his mom who had pointed it out, clamped onto the curved edge of the canoe. It was awful. The bug's back was split and something bright and terribly green was crawling out of itself. He watched while his stomach turned. His mother explained that the cicada would dry and harden, that its new exoskeleton would be larger than the last, and that that's how some insects grew. But it just looked incredibly painful. The teenager Cal was then couldn't figure out at what point the old cicada stopped being and the new cicada became. The adult Cal flicked the discarded carcass off the chair before he sat down to eat breakfast with Tracy.

After they were done eating (the dogs had been mostly good, only doing their quiet begging by lying at Cal and Tracy's feet), Cal offered Stella a leftover bit of bacon from his plate. She approached slowly, took it soft-mouthed and looked up at him with her amber eyes, lit by the morning sun. She pulled her head back and spit the bacon on the ground, where Smoke quickly lunged for it and gobbled it down.

The guy next to Cal ordered another beer, and said to no one in particular, "Jesus, it was hot today."

Cal grunted in agreement, and signaled to the bartender for another beer. Luke was running late. There was a small pile of crumpled and torn beer labels on the bar in front of the guy who'd clearly had more than a couple.

"You work out by the lake?" he asked, rubbing the back of his neck.

"Today," Cal answered. "I kind of work all over."

"I do landscaping, a lot of work on those rich people's lawns," he continued. "I'd like to get a little more." He took a sip of his beer, took his hat off where his hair was cut short around a balding spot, and put it back on. "You know the Luft place?"

"Not really," Cal said.

He hadn't been out there or met Tracy's parents. Other than that conversation about Aaron when she'd first returned from Idaho, they hadn't really talked about her family, but he knew which place was theirs. By the standards of some of those mansions, they had a smaller house, but some of the best frontage on the lake, all perfectly manicured down to the lake, with a well-kept seawall and a couple piers. Growing up there must have been idyllic – or at least seemed that way.

"I wouldn't mind getting back on that property. I was once and I sure do miss it," the man said, finishing his beer.

Cal saw Luke come in the side door and waved to catch his eye. Luke stopped for a minute and blinked, then started walking toward Cal.

As he passed behind the man in the hat, who was just getting up from the padded stool, Luke said under his breath, "What're you doing, Greg?"

Cal heard him and stiffened. Luke took the newly-vacated stool and watched the man head for the door, a little slowly and carefully, with a slight waver.

"Do you know who that was?" he asked Cal.

"I do now."

Part Three: August

Greg

In the first week of August, the county was mowing down all the weeds and grass that had grown tall along the edges of the roads; the bright bursts of blue-purple that were mostly chicory, the breezy heads of wild carrot. Those too-long, too-dense weeds obscured the view from side roads and provided cover for small mammals and deer before they crossed the road. Greg's business was only private mowing, not driving the big county machines, but he did his own share of cutting down the chicory and wild carrot from private properties. On the smaller mowers, he could see what else he cut, too – all the milkweed and nettle and clover – so he knew what all that mowing was likely doing to the local butterfly populations.

Early August and even the highway roadsides were beautiful, despite the salt that poisoned most of the soil there. But all anyone seemed to see was the way the plants were tall and ungainly.

Chicory root could be ground and drunk instead of coffee or added to coffee to give it a distinctive New Orleans-style taste. Nettles were delicious. Greg liked to have them with his pasta. And wild carrot roots were edible when young. It seemed like most things that were a *thing*, like beards or polenta or nettles (in cities, hipsters ate them) were just poor people's foods or fashions or country people's customs that had been 're-discovered' by people who weren't poor or country. If Greg sold what he foraged by the ounce in some place that had more than one zip code, he thought he could probably make a good living.

When he was little, his grandfather pointed out the tiny, brown-red spot in the center of the wild-carrot flower, and told him why it was called Queen Anne's lace. Queen Anne was making lace (like his grandmother did, *tatting*), using fine silk thread and a slim needle, and pricked her finger and a single spot of blood fell onto the delicate lace. Now all the flower heads, once they got big and showy enough, would have a single blood spot for Queen Anne.

Both Greg's grandparents died before he was ten, but he remembered how his grandfather told him stories as they would walk the fields behind their house, collecting plants, and then cook with what they found. The first few years he and Tracy were together, he'd tell her the stories, too. He thought it would always be like this, passing those stories down; that some-day he'd maybe tell his kids, and that way someone would know what chicory was for and where to find the mushrooms, and where the fish waited when the sun got too hot.

For a while, the story of Queen Anne got confused in his head and Greg forgot what his grandfather had told him. He started thinking of the story of some other queen (maybe one of the queens who were beheaded by their husbands, probably for infidelity or for not providing an heir, or any other sin that the king judged to be worthy of this most serious of punishments). So when he'd gather a handful of lacy heads of wild carrot, he wasn't thinking of his gentle grandfather and his sweet grandmother, but of Tracy and what she'd done to him.

Sure, she'd left him the house but she'd taken the business, his livelihood, which left him no way to pay the taxes and insurance and the note on the remaining land. He'd had to sell off most of it, and could only keep the little parcel where the house stood. Now his woods were being cut down, and people were putting up cheap, vinyl-sided houses in full view of his house. He'd lost even the peace and quiet. He'd had to start over from scratch with no money, trying to scrape enough together for a few mowers, taking on work with the local township plowing roads in the winter, where a big part of his job was depositing the toxic mix of salt and mineral additives onto the road that poisoned the land. It made him sick. At least he'd had some effect lately, arguing for sanding and a better mix that included some sugar-beet byproduct that was supposed to be less harmful to groundwater and soil.

If he and Tracy were still together (the old Tracy who actually gave a fuck about him), she'd know how hurtful it was that he was a part of this slow process of poisoning the roadsides. Even the landscaping business and those goddamned rich people by the lake (people like Tracy's parents) required him to use a cocktail of chemicals that ran off into the lake. He tried to talk to people about the unnecessary phosphorus in most fertilizer, the dangers of algae blooms. Jesus, it smelled like leather – didn't that tell them any-thing? Their kids and dogs couldn't even go on the grass for three days. But they just smiled past him, their stupid gardener, and told him to carry on. Luckily, the state legislature had caught on and passed some regulation, but the rich people just did what they wanted for their picture-perfect lawns, offering him extra to use their "special mix" on the lawn, proffering a hand-ful of cash. (Usually he needed the cash.)

The day that Tracy found out about him and that woman and got in her car and drove away, he knew he'd fucked up bad but he didn't think that that would be the last time he'd see her, the last time he'd talk to her; that from then on, she'd communicate with him only via certified letters, typed by her lawyer's secretary. He thought that once she'd cooled down, he'd have a chance to explain (or, if not to explain, at least to apologize).

What he never got to say was how much it hurt him how she'd been withdrawing from him that year; that every day she snuck out of bed early and pretended that that was not what she was doing was also a betrayal; that maybe she wasn't fucking someone else (but it was almost as bad); that all those years the one thing they'd always had was the way they'd been together when they'd been alone; that that had been the one place where it hadn't mattered that she was richer and smarter and had gone to college and everyone knew she could do a lot better than him; that knowing he could touch her and bring her off and make her happy, again and again, was the one way he felt equal to her, that he was worthy of her. The house and the business felt like the beginning of a life they were building together where who his parents were and who her parents were didn't matter. Every time she moved away from him and *then lied,* as if he wouldn't get it, was another time she was saying to him that he was *too stupid* to get it. Maybe he'd done the most unforgiveable thing but she had done some unforgiveable things, too. Whatever had been broken, they'd both broken it.

He never even cared about that woman.

When Greg heard that Aaron had died, he thought that maybe now he and Tracy could talk. Sometimes losing someone made people realize they'd made a mistake. Greg was planning to give it a couple of weeks, then give her a call, or stop by casually, to express his condolences – but then he'd heard about the new guy. This new guy wasn't the passing-through, one-night-stand kind of guy she'd used over the past two years. (Yeah, he'd kept track. Not hard in a small town when the ex-girlfriend's house is across from the gas station. It's hard not to look across the street and see things.) When he was working at the neighbor's property out on the lake, Tracy's father even waved and said hello to him – so it's not like there weren't signs telling him to give it a try. But he didn't plan that at Salty's, that guy sitting down next to him; he was minding his own business. That guy should have known who he was.

Everybody knew who everybody was. His grandfather had been dead for more than almost thirty years and still people would stop him sometimes and ask him if he was Spook's grandson. His grandfather had been constable for the next township, served on the village board, and had known and treated everyone well. The local bars had dart tournaments and the rotating trophy was the Spook Trophy. All Greg had to do was stop down by the local chapter of the Veterans of Foreign Wars to hear stories about his grandfather, about how his grandmother made the best potato salad for the annual summer picnic (she thinly diced up her own sweet pickles, used a special spice recipe). It hadn't mattered that they didn't have money, or weren't successful or college-educated. Just like Greg's grandfather used to say: *I don't care how much you know, I know how much you care.*

The Piggly Wiggly was laid out like most other grocery stores: produce on the one edge, meat and dairy at the far end, a small end cap with local brats and cheeses. Greg had cut out from work a little early, the skies threatening rain, and stopped for a few groceries, maybe something to grill alongside the zucchini in his garden that were getting too big and would be inedible soon. He was pushing his cart down the cereal aisle when he saw Tracy at the deli counter getting two-pound containers of potato salad, talking to a woman in a hairnet. He wasn't surprised because she never was much of a cook – but she must be going somewhere for dinner, or having someone over. He turned his cart around to stay out of sight and waited at the end of the pet food aisle, knowing she'd be heading there soon. Her new dogs were intimidating-looking, and he'd wondered if her getting them meant she knew he'd been stopping by. By accident though, he'd met the two pit bulls. They weren't really aggressive, and seemed eager for any kind of attention once he threw a few treats over the fence – the other one, not so much.

Sure enough, Tracy loaded two twenty-pound bags of kibble into her cart, a couple of pouches of treats, and then headed to the registers. He figured he could finish his shopping later; he left his cart and skirted the edge of the store to make it to the parking lot before she did. He watched her load most of the bags into her hatchback (so it would look like he'd just casually walked up when she started to lug the first bag of dog food into her arms). As she lifted the weight of the bag, the cart moved on its wheels. He reached for it and she looked up.

She didn't seem to recognize him at first, just smiled her bland stranger smile at him. He knew he'd changed a little: his hair shorter, his thin spot sunburned and shining in the late afternoon sun. But how could she not recognize his walk, or the way his hands gripped the cart's handle, his scarred knuckles, the hands that used to touch her. He would recognize her silhouetted shadow a hundred yards away. He pretended to be surprised that it was her.

"Oh. Hi, Tracy," he fake stammered.

"Greg." Full stop, the end of a sentence. She hefted a bag of dog food into the car, crushing some of her grocery bags.

"Let me help you," he offered.

"I've got it." She quickly grabbed the second bag and piled it on top of the first. Greg's fabricated reason for being there, for stopping, was gone and she turned away.

"Tracy?" She turned back for a moment. "I'm sorry to hear about Aaron..." and he saw a shadow of pain cross her face. He was saddened to have caused this pain but also knew this might be his only opportunity to make her listen. But her face closed again and she looked past him. She slammed the hatchback and began to push the cart across the asphalt to the cart corral. He put out his hand and stopped the cart, stopped her.

"Tracy, can we talk for a minute?" He made his voice sound soft, pleading. He needed her to stop moving, to listen. Maybe in his voice she'd remember the times Aaron had come over, had sat at their table. Greg made tea for them, or fussed around in the kitchen just off the dining table, giving space but signaling he was there, he was always there – if they needed him.

"No." She broke the cart free from his grasp, stalked across the lane and pushed it hard until it hit the other carts, locking into alignment. She walked past him, and accidentally brushed his shoulder. He felt her recoil.

"Trace!" And now he said the name he used to call her and he was angry. "I don't understand why we can't be friends." She stopped, standing ready to pull the handle on her car, and turned and looked at him.

"I can think of a reason," she said, got into her car, and drove away.

Conversation

Thankfully, the spot in front of her was empty so she could just pull ahead. She was too angry and flustered to deal with the careful checking of the rearview mirror and backing up before leaving the small parking lot. She knew Greg would be standing there, watching her drive away, as she pulled out of the lot. She didn't bother to yield for oncoming traffic either, as she pulled out onto the road. She had been excited and looking forward to the evening: picking up Stella and taking her out to Lucy's to try the agility equipment, having dinner with Lucy and Carla. First she had to pull over on a side street to calm down, breathe in and out and collect herself. She hit the steering wheel a few times with her fists, forgetting to watch her hands and accidentally hitting the horn, startling herself and probably the neighbors.

She drove past the county fairgrounds, past the padlocked gates, where a road crew stood around two trucks, shovels in hand, wearing fluorescent orange vests, even though they were safely sequestered from traffic and passing cars. They were patching the long strip of asphalt that would be the Midway soon, the gathering for the games and rides and food trucks. The smell of hot tar and road patch filtered into Tracy's car.

Once, a summer between college semesters, Tracy had applied to work on a road crew with the county; imagined herself orange-vested, turning the poled sign from Stop to Slow. She'd walked into the highway department, past the men smoking on their break, their forearms showing raised, red welts from the arc of hot tar. She didn't get the job. Tracy had been fed two fictions: that this place was her home, and that this place was somewhere she'd escape from easily, like sloughing off a sweater when the weather got warm.

Tracy loved the county fair with its flicker of lights and crush of smells and sounds and bodies. As a kid, the whole family would go, except her father, who was often working and, if he wasn't, still wasn't interested in the fair. Tracy liked the big rides: the Rock-o-Planes and the Scrambler. Sometimes they'd all go on the Tilt-a-Whirl, but afterward her mother would walk slowly with a strange look on her face and have to sit for a while at the 4-H tent to sip water while her stomach settled. The family vote always ended the same way (her mother and Aaron against her), so they'd go first to the small animal barn, and pet the rabbits between the wires of their cages, remark on the strange plumage of exotic fowl. Only afterward could they go to the large animal barns, Tracy's favorites.

She loved the sheep, petting their curly coats, full or shorn. Some wore homemade blankets, sewn with leftover scraps or made to match, to identify these animals as some unlikely family mascots. When she was little, Tracy liked to guess what it was about the sheep that earned the ribbons hung on the back of their stalls. She'd stare into the animals' eyes: liquid and deep and imagine they were having some sort of conversation. She'd watch the judging: teen boys and girls leading their animals to the judges; the judges checking muscle and bone, fat and meat, assessing bodies and breeding and awarding blue ribbons or red ribbons or nothing at all.

That was when Tracy realized what the accolades meant – the prize-winning animals would be bought and slaughtered first. Those eyes she had been gazing into were destined for the long, last drive to the local slaughterhouse. If the stock was fine enough, maybe the prestige would pass on to their offspring, to others of their flock, guaranteeing a business of the flesh for years to come. When she and Greg were together, they'd buy a lamb each year (Greg said if they were going to eat meat, it might as well be local) and have the whole animal butchered and portioned, packed neatly into their chest freezer.

When Tracy got home, she unloaded the groceries, and got out the head halters to take Smoke and Red for a walk. She'd been planning to anyway, before she and Stella headed out to Lucy's. Now the walk would help calm her down. How dare he bring up Aaron. If he really wanted to express his condolences, he could have sent a card, like any normal person. Greg was like those realtors who read a death notice in the paper, noted the address, and sent a letter that began with "Sorry to hear of your loss," then quickly segued to a mention of their sales figures and how they'd be happy to represent the sale of the property. Her parents had gotten these after Aaron's obituary appeared in the local paper. Vultures.

With the dogs' thin tails whipping and their happiness at the walk, it was hard to stay angry, though. This was what always surprised Tracy: how the dogs' moods were infectious and how easy it was for their happiness to become her own. What she had planned to be a short walk, around four blocks, stretched longer – across the railroad tracks and behind the school's track and football field. The summer mowers were out and soon they'd be painting stripes on the field to make ten-yard lengths, the junior varsity and varsity teams practicing in the afternoons after morning weight training.

In another week, Tracy would begin going into the office mid-morning, preparing schedules and paperwork for the coming school year. It always snuck up on her that June and July passed so quickly, so she tried to pack a whole summer into the beginning of August. Tomorrow, she'd go out on a pontoon boat with Cal and his sister.

As she turned onto her street, the dogs were starting to slow down and she knew they'd sleep well, snoring on the couch, while she and Stella were gone that night. It hadn't rained after all, and she'd need to get up early tomorrow and water plants before she left for the lake. She'd also need to spend some time planning which swimsuit to wear in front of Cal and his family, to pick something flattering but demure, something that wouldn't fall off if they went tubing or kneeboarding. If it was just she and Cal, she would've worn her string bikini. As she got older, Tracy thought she looked better the less she wore, and never understood why women tended to wear more and more layers, and shapewear, squeezing themselves into spandex and lycra, looking like sausage casings. Tracy liked her curves, her soft spots. She liked the way she looked in a bikini, even better how she looked with nothing on at all. After she moved to town, one of the things she missed was that she couldn't walk around naked whenever she wanted, just wearing her own skin. She didn't know Cal's sister Deena well at all, but what little she did know gave her the idea she'd have to wear at least a tankini. Cal had told her that it was Deena who had suggested he ask Tracy out; she'd used words like "respectable" to describe her. It must have been because Tracy was well-spoken, or the family she came from.

Deena was a certain kind of respectable: chair of the PTA, the Booster Club, and highly visible at every bake sale and planning committee since her children had entered elementary school. She was one of those stay-at-home moms whose presence caused audible groans in the district office whenever she was spotted approaching the sliding-glass window. Her older boy had had a few discipline problems, her younger girl, too (although Tracy suspected these had more to do with the girl not behaving in stereotypical, feminine ways). Deena would argue her way out of almost any consequence, wearing the assistant principal down with phone calls and meetings until he waited out her children aging out of the small elementary school. Since they'd both moved on to the middle school, everyone had been more than happy to be nice-as-pie to Deena whenever she stopped in with another "great idea" for a combined school event. Since Tracy didn't have the long history of interactions with Deena the Super Mom, the other administrative staff greatly appreciated her handling these visits.

It was sometimes whispered that Deena had to get married, that the older boy had arrived within months of the wedding, but given the fervor with which Deena threw herself into wifedom and motherhood, these whispers were half-hearted by now. When Tracy asked about his sister, Cal had sighed a little, and described her as "a force." It was Deena who had called to invite Tracy boating. They had a pontoon. "Adults only," she gushed; just she and her husband and a couple of friends. Tracy had agreed before she'd checked with Cal and realized Deena hadn't even mentioned it to him yet. When she asked what she could bring, Deena told her not to trouble herself, just bring whatever she wanted to drink. Cal suggested they might need to pack some hard liquor.

Tracy was thinking of all this as she thought about the contrast between her two social activities – the all-female rescue farm picnic, then the boating with Cal and his force-of-a-sister and her friends. She fed the pits, gave Stella half her usual portion, loaded her into the car, locked the gate, and headed out of town (the store-bought potato salad transferred into a glass bowl so it might pass for homemade).

Stella did well on the agility equipment, and Tracy's mood improved, the memory of Greg receding. Watching slow Stella amble up to poles and jump them, her baggy skin moving in slow motion was comic relief for Lucy and Carla. Sarah, who Tracy remembered as the vet tech, came out from the barn to watch, giggling under her breath. The tunnel took some coaxing, but eventually Stella did that too, despite the fact that it got caught on her haunches and she dragged it around the yard a bit before Lucy could detach it. The only obstacles she wouldn't try were the A-Frame and the Teeter-Totter. But Tracy couldn't blame her for that. After introducing them, Lucy had their border collie, Goose, and Jake, the cocker spaniel-mix, demonstrate, but Stella would stop at the base of each of these apparatuses, and swing her large head toward Tracy, as if to enquire whether she'd lost her mind. The big dog would snort, wander away, and lie down.

Tracy really enjoyed showing off Stella's skills with the off-leash hand signals. As much as her responses were slower, she followed Tracy's pointing fingers and upheld flat palms, duly stopping and waiting, sitting, and walk-running wherever directed. Two months ago, Stella thought Tracy was the interloper, and now it seemed like the woman and the dog were of the same mind. Watching Stella do this work and play and relax with the other dogs made Tracy think of her brother briefly, but thankfully, for this gift he had given her.

When Sarah called the horses in, and they caught sight of Stella, their reaction was another show. They began bucking and kicking all over the paddock, wild for a moment, and both Carla and Lucy stopped to watch.

"I was wondering how the horses would react to her," Lucy said, calling for Sarah to come out of the barn and see. After a few minutes of their antics, the horses were lined up on the other side of the fence, standing calmly in front of Stella. She was standing too, facing them, head lowered, with her shoulders thrown forward. They seemed to be engaged in a staring contest.

"What are they doing?" Sarah asked.

"Did you read up on the Bordeaux's history at all?" Lucy asked Tracy.

"A little..." Tracy said, "but I don't know what that is."

"They were guard dogs, but also all around working dogs, too. Some were used on farms, to herd cattle, and as drovers," Lucy continued. "I believe they might be having a conversation about moving animals, or Stella is trying to move those horses."

"Maybe we could use her with Thelma," Sarah interjected.

"That probably would not be a good idea," Carla laughed. "Call her off, Tracy."

After Sarah finished in the barn, they all sat down to eat. It was a feast of salads and black bean and sweet potato burgers, watermelon, and sun tea that had been steeping all day; Tracy felt downright healthy. The three dogs all waited for scraps and the four women settled into easy conversation about their plans for the weekend and the future. With the dogs easing the tension, Sarah was able to make friends with Stella, ending up with drool shellacking her legs. Carla and Lucy were excited to have had their plans approved for the pool and shared their wedding plans, too.

When Tracy mentioned that this was the first cookout she'd been to in a while without either brats or beer (usually brats boiled first in beer), Carla told some stories about how hard it was for her and Lucy to go out. Wisconsin supper clubs celebrated two things: meat and cocktails. Lucy ended up eating off the kids' menu most of the time (grilled cheese), and most people looked down their nose at anyone who didn't drink. Sometimes Carla'd order a seltzer with lime, just so it would look like she was having a gin and tonic or something. Tracy wasn't trying to pry, but Carla didn't seem to mind talking about why she didn't drink: about her father who was a bad drunk and abusive, or about when she realized that most of her happy memories (including the first few years with Lucy) were a little hazy because she'd had a few too many. Lucy put her hand over Carla's at that moment, touching her fingertips gently, gingerly, then diffused the moment.

"That's probably why she asked me to marry her," Lucy said, laughing. "Living on a horse farm in Iowa. Beer goggles."

Carla squeezed her hand then, but looked a little pained; it passed quickly.

"I kept asking you, though," she reminded her. "And I've been sober a long time."

Tracy tried to change the subject, asking Sarah how long she'd been helping with the animals, asking about the falling-down barn beyond the pole building (it had been there since before they bought the place, Carla told her, leftover from the old homestead).

"We've been thinking it would make a nice guest cottage," Carla said, "for when my sister comes to visit, maybe." It needed a lot of work, but had some beautiful wood, and an old stone foundation that stretched about a third of the way up the exterior. In its current state of disrepair, most people would let it fall apart, or tear it down.

"If you're interested, I might know someone for the job," Tracy offered, helping herself to a second burger. "These are good, by the way," she directed to Lucy.

"Any chance this 'somebody' is the person who appreciates the dog-free room?" Lucy asked, smiling. Tracy blushed.

"Maybe." She took a bite of her burger.

"I heard he does nice stonework," Lucy continued. "Oh! I forgot. We got some pickles at work today!" She ran into the house and came out with a mason jar, popped it open. "Did you remember to bring yours home, Sarah?"

"Um huh," Sarah answered, mid-bite of a watermelon slice, the curve of the fruit giving her a cartoonish smile.

"Who's that from?" Carla asked.

"Eckstrands. We euthanized their cat, and they couldn't pay the whole bill. They brought us all pickles and freezer jam," Sarah answered. Sarah had spent a lot of time with their cat lately. And when the Eckstrands couldn't bear to be there, they'd handed their cat over to Sarah and nodded ever so slightly, as they left the exam room.

"Did you all make a decision about the Lawson dog?" Carla asked quietly, of both Lucy and Sarah.

The younger woman's eyes flicked to Tracy, "I called." Carla nodded, went back to her meal.

The Lake

Tracy hadn't been out on the lake all summer. Between the Idaho trip, the fixes to the house, and the dogs, she just hadn't taken the time and now she realized she'd been missing it. She loved to swim, to sun herself, to dive from the boat into the deep lake where the water was always cool. Some people preferred the smaller lakes where there were sandy beaches, where people could slowly walk out and swim. Although the big lake was rocky along its shore and weedy in places, it was one of the deepest, inland lakes in the whole state; the water was always clear and cold, without some of the algae issues that seemed to plague shallower waters. There was nothing better than jumping into that water on a hot day.

Cal picked her up, and she added her six-pack to his cooler of ice. As promised, he'd pre-measured tequila into a bottle of margarita mix, and packed an open sleeve of plastic cups. It wouldn't be fancy, he apologized – no cut limes or salted rims, but depending on how the day went, he thought they might need a drink. He'd also brought a couple bags of chips, baby carrots and dip, and a container of raspberries.

"Deena got the boat for the whole eight hours," he said on the way over, sounding tired already.

"You aren't looking forward to it?" Tracy asked.

"Eight hours is a long time with my sister."

"We could tie up and stop at a bar for lunch," she smiled. "If you're hitting that tequila, you should probably eat a burger or something."

Tracy had slept so well last night, and she thought maybe it was because she hadn't had anything to drink. It had been a long time since she hadn't even had a beer or two before going to bed. Partly that was summer, partly that was Deb, and partly that was growing up a good Wisconsin girl from a household where drinking was just the norm. Her parents always had a drink or two before dinner, wine with dinner and, pretty often, a cognac after dinner. She always thought that this was what everyone did, but remembered going home for Thanksgiving with a friend in college and bringing a bottle of wine as a 'Thank you' for her hosts. But they didn't drink and hadn't quite known what to do. They put the wine out with the meal, but Tracy had been the only one who poured some for herself and she'd felt embarrassed. Later, she'd tried to think what else a person would bring when going to someone else's house for dinner. She couldn't think of a single thing – bread? That seemed cheap. Should she have brought some Wisconsin cheese? That seemed cliché. That she couldn't think of anything else to bring, couldn't even go one meal without wine, seemed to say something about her, and not something good. It just didn't feel like dinner if there wasn't some kind of alcohol.

But the dinner with Lucy and Carla and Sarah had been lovely, and she hadn't missed having a beer in her hand. And she hadn't slept that well in so long she couldn't remember. She even slept through Stella's pacing, something the dog had taken to doing lately, getting up in the middle of the night and making the rounds of the windows, making her chuffing noises. She remembered the bed shaking as the dog left for her nightly rounds, but she drifted right back to sleep, and must have slept through Stella's return, like Smoke and Red did, snoring on the couch, ignoring Stella's overactive imagination.

She woke up this morning thinking maybe she'd stop drinking so much. But a beer on a pontoon boat, the lake water shimmering, and the sun beating down until it was so hot she had to jump in, made for a perfect summer day, so that resolution only lasted as long as it took for Cal to pull up with the blue and white cooler already packed with ice, with room left for her addition. Besides, she trusted his estimation of his sister; she'd probably need the beers.

In the end, it wasn't Deena who was so bad – she was at least trying to be sensitive to Tracy. But her friends, a couple from high school, seemed only to have come along to gawk at the lake houses and throw barbs at the people who owned them. Tracy tried to interject from time to time, pointing out that many of the biggest estates were actually owned by corporations, not families, who used them as retreats and bonuses for their executives, but it didn't really matter. From the vantage point of the lake, those sprawling lawns and hand-laid stone steps all led to boat houses that were bigger than their own home. The houses must all be owned by terrible people: trust-fund babies and stock market assholes. It didn't help that a bunch of the beautiful wooden boats had names like *Read the Fine Print* or *Second Option*.

Of course, they were passing Tracy's parent's house when the husband started to get particularly animated, actually pulling down his shorts and mooning the couple sitting on the end of their pier. They weren't close enough to make out faces, but it had to be her parents. Deena, offended by this lack of decorum (and also fully aware whose house it was), yelled at the guy to stop it, shooting a quick glance at Tracy.

"Why the hell should I? Fucking FIBs!" he retorted, raising his voice and flipping off the couple who appeared to be getting up and making their way back up their dock.

"Those are my parents," Tracy said, "and they live here, always have," as if what he was upset about was their primary zip code. His wife put her hand on her husband's arm and pulled him down until he was sitting.

The wife turned to Tracy, grimacing, "I'm sorry, Tracy, we didn't know..."

"It's OK. My dad is kind of an asshole, but I think my mom's alright." She finished her beer, opened the cooler for another. "If we go over to the cliffs on the other side, we can swim up to the caves." She nodded across the lake where the sandstone stood up about one hundred feet above the water.

Deena stayed with the boat, with what's-her-name's husband, but every-one else swam to the bluff, where they gingerly walked up to the little caves made in the sandstone, pockets, and depressions from the waves over how-ever many years. Most of the lake was too deep for any anchor, so someone had to stay with the boat anyway, motoring against the current. As they looked at the thick layers of spider webs and a large black spider, a hands-breadth across, Cal tapped her on the shoulder and nodded in the direction of the boat where it looked like Deena was giving her guest a talking-to, furiously gesticulating, the man sitting on one of the padded benches, head down, staring at the floor. They exchanged a smile, just as they saw his wife catch the scene on the boat.

"I really am sorry Tracy," she said. "He's had a few beers."

"Don't worry. I grew up here. I'm used to it." Tracy did feel bad for the woman. She kind of wished she'd mentioned that she'd grown up on the lake, or that Deena had given them a head's up, so the awkwardness could have been avoided. The only other awkwardness had to do with a second mention of the house, this time Deena's. They were circling the lakeshore, doubling back by Tracy's parent's house.

"So that'll be yours someday," Deena said to Tracy, but not really looking at her.

"Um, I guess."

Tracy hadn't really thought of this. She'd spent so long separating herself from her parents and their life that she hadn't thought about the physical inheritance of the house. Underlying Deena's comment was also Aaron's death, and it was this casual knowledge that Deena seemed to just throw out there, that seemed most hurtful.

The other woman, Asshole's wife, asked, "Do you have brothers and sisters Tracy?" completely innocently, and Deena shot her a look, as if she was the one being inappropriate.

Cal answered. "Tracy's brother died earlier this year," and he took Tracy's hand, turned angry eyes on his sister.

Deena had been bugging him a lot lately about him and Tracy, about how it was going, fishing for details, in a way that was a little overeager, a little more than idle curiosity. But even he was surprised by the comment about her inheriting the house. He knew she was imagining some happy future: he and Tracy together at that house, inviting them over for summer days of family gatherings and swimming and boating, their own pontoon tied up on the dock, not having to rent a boat and split the day's costs like the regular townies.

When Deena had called Cal to tell him about the plans for Saturday, he'd already been pissed that she'd invited Tracy without bothering to mention it to him first. Then she'd told him his cost for the day would be $125 plus a share of gas. She'd told him not to mention it to Tracy, that she didn't want her to think they were renting the boat. Didn't she think, he'd asked her, that Tracy would figure it out when they showed up at the public dock? She'd called him a smartass then, but said *Of course, it's not like we're keeping it from her, but we just don't need to make a big deal of it, little brother.* When he found out who the other couple was, he was even more worried, but by then Tracy had already said yes, and told Cal she was looking forward to it – that she hadn't been out on a boat all summer. He couldn't decide whether to warn her or not, so he didn't say anything.

There were a lot of things lately that he couldn't figure out whether to tell Tracy, so in the end he didn't say anything. He hadn't told her about running into Greg, or the weird thing he'd said about getting back on *that property*. He hadn't told her how uncomfortable he still was with Stella, that she hadn't just cornered him in the bathroom (Tracy knew that), but had poked him in a way that seemed particularly pointed – a pretty clear message. And there were other things he hadn't told her because he didn't even know how to articulate what he meant to himself. These were the kind of things Deena had been asking about, too – and he'd tensed (because it was his big sister butting in and meddling like she liked to, because he didn't know how to answer her anyway, and because it pissed him off that Deena was right about most things).

For the last two years, Deena had been working part-time at a local realtor's, learning about the lake, its areas, the ratio of feet of frontage to dollars, the average increase in tax assessments. While they were ringing the less prosperous side of the lake between the two disastrous passes by Tracy's parent's house, where the houses were just regular homes (mostly two or three bedrooms), she was tallying sales prices and estimating insurance and taxes. She thought that once the kids left for college that they'd maybe be able to afford something over here, or maybe a lake view with shared access over by the bluffs. If it came with a slip, it might be worth it. For now, Deena was making connections she could use later.

When Deena got knocked up on her second date by the guy she'd ended up marrying (who was now a great husband and father, but then was a high school drop-out, just some local mechanic she was killing time with), she set to work on this new project like it had always been part of the plan. Through her own sheer force of will – a will that quite frankly scared Cal when he saw what it could do – she'd organized her own wedding and marriage in a way that had made most people forget that any of it wasn't what she'd originally wanted out of life.

First, the now-fiancé got his GED before the wedding. After their son was born, Deena got her new husband to take some night classes at the tech and finish an associates in business management. He ended up working his way up until he owned a garage. He still built engines but, just as often, wore a button-down with his name stitched-on that didn't need weekly cleaning for grease stains. Deena stayed home with the kids, but also took in a few other people's kids (staying under the number that would require inspections and licensing), adding to the family budget. They bought a manufactured home, landscaped around the base to hide its origins, got a black lab, and a Camry. When Deena said that a person can do anything he puts his mind to, she meant it. She meant that a person can learn to love someone and build a life, if he wants to – she was the proof. Lately she'd been saying this a lot.

What Needed to be Done

The Eckstrands' cat must have been at least twenty-years-old. They'd adopted it when it was an adult cat from a local shelter and they'd had it for eighteen years. For the last six years, it had had a wound on its front leg that wouldn't heal. They'd brought it in and Dr. Larsen had tried everything he could think of: several rounds of antibiotics and anti-inflammatories and needle biopsies that were inconclusive, but they'd declined putting the cat under anesthesia for exploratory surgery. By now, it seemed to be a behavioral issue. The cat worried the spot, chewed open the skin, and they'd return home to blood spatter on the walls, blood soaked into the couch and bedding. The injury didn't seem to affect its gait and, otherwise, the cat seemed fine. For the last year, they'd taken to wrapping the front leg so it couldn't get to it, changing the dressing every couple of days.

Old cats look sad. And lately, Clavin (named after the character from the sitcom *Cheers*) had stopped being able to clean himself well, and had developed other problems around the litterbox. When he stopped playing and started hiding most of the time, they brought him back to the vet, and in addition to his long-term leg wound, terrible teeth, and arthritis, he was diagnosed with end-stage chronic kidney disease. Sarah sat down to talk with the Eckstrands.

Veterinary care had changed lately, along with the cultural changes that tended to include pets in the notion of 'family.' Christmas cards featured pets as often as they featured children. Pet boutiques popped up alongside clothing stores for people. 'Pet parents' scheduled regular dental care for their pets. Changes like these were slower to catch on in small towns, and Sarah was glad for this. Although their clinic offered dental care, many of their clients stared at them blank-faced when they offered these services, or when they were asked how often they brushed their dogs' teeth. Secretly, this made Sarah happy. Although she wanted the animals to have the best possible care, she sympathized with the clients who refused this aspect of their service, pointing out that they themselves didn't even have dental insurance, so why would they spend money regularly on dental cleaning for their pets. Philosophically, Sarah thought that going into debt, doing whatever is possible for an animal – even a greatly beloved animal – was often wrongheaded. And this was how Sarah found her niche.

During her first week working at the clinic on Prospect Street, a young woman had come in to return some medication for her Great Dane, Hershey. Her dog had been behaving strangely after dinner, and when she'd called their emergency line, Dr. Larsen had told her to get her dog to the emergency clinic in Oshkosh as fast as she could. The dog was bloating, a common occurrence in large breeds, and needed immediate care. She got to the emergency clinic in time, but the dog's stomach had twisted and the animal was in shock; it needed immediate surgery, but the cost of surgery, aftercare, and two nights stay was over four thousand dollars. She couldn't afford it, so she euthanized her dog. With the x-rays, fluids and final cocktail, that still came to over eight hundred dollars.

She was returning some leftover heartworm medication to get a little money back. When she told Dr. Larsen about Hershey, she was gripping the top of the counter and looking down to avoid eye contact, her eyes welling. As he took the still-closed boxes from her, he said, "And you wouldn't pay it?"

Sarah tried not to gasp. At eight, Hershey was already old for a Great Dane. Even with the surgery, he might not have lived for more than another year or two. Sarah didn't know if the woman ever got another dog, or just found another vet, but she remembered that after the woman walked out of the clinic, she sat in the front seat of her car for a long time before she finally pulled out of the lot.

While Sarah may not have been able to put animals out of their misery when she was younger, what she could do was listen to the clients who couldn't afford anything and everything for their pets, and tell them that it was OK. She could tell them that prolonging life for the sake of a few more days, weeks, or even a few more months, isn't always the right thing to do. She could tell them that deciding when it's time to euthanize (she didn't care for euphemisms and wouldn't say "put down" or "put to sleep") is the most important part of being a pet owner, of loving a pet. And for those people who couldn't be there, who couldn't face the act themselves, she told them she would be there for them; that she would hold their cat or dog, sit with them, and talk to them until it was done.

She spent a lot of time in the back room, holding animals, or sitting next to cages, stroking fur, and talking to animals she didn't know. She'd carry their warm, still bodies to wherever they needed to go, depending on whether the person had asked for the remains back, or for individual or group cremation. She felt useful. No one else wanted to do this part of the job.

So when the Eckstrands came in the last time, they'd already done some research, read about dialysis and kidney transplants, but ended with "Clavin is so old," Sarah said that maybe it was time to consider euthanasia. She said this before Dr. Larsen could come in and suggest other treatments, other options. Mr. and Mrs. Eckstrand were also old, retired, and drawing on their social security. They always paid their bill with a credit card – a different one each time (Donna had pointed it out), and Sarah thought that they probably had trouble paying their vet bills already. Clavin was in Mrs. Eckstrand's lap, looking deflated, his eyes gummy with reddish discharge staining his buff-colored fur. Mr. Eckstrand was stroking him, and the oily sheen of his coat made each vertebrae stick out and look like a partially-deboned fish carcass. Mr. Eckstrand nodded and Mrs. Eckstrand swallowed.

Dennis was a different story – a dog they worked very hard to save. He was a yorkie-mix, about five years old, whose chest had been torn open by the Lawson's dog. They stabilized him as best they could, called the Oshkosh clinic, and sent him off to the full surgery suite. In the meantime, the Lawson woman came in, waving her credit card, assuring everyone she'd pay for anything "little Dennis" needed, including any and all aftercare. She asked them to call the emergency clinic, explain the situation, and "make the arrangements." Dennis was all of six pounds. He'd need major surgery to repair the damage from the initial attack and the secondary scuffle, when the Lawson dog slipped its harness, picked him up a second time, and shook him by the neck.

The Lawson dog was a coonhound-pit mix, unvaccinated and unlicensed. It had attacked at least one other dog, whose bills had also been paid for. There were other dog scuffles that hadn't needed stitches. Each time, Mrs. Lawson (who was not a client of theirs) begged the victim not to call the police, not to report her dog. She made it worth their while, and people who loved their dogs understood when she broke down in tears, explaining how much she needed her dog, how she couldn't bear it if she had to put her dog down.

The first time it happened, everyone at the clinic sympathized and grudgingly went along, but apparently she continued to tell people her dog was "friendly," that it just wanted to "make friends." She left her dog tied up out in front of her house, on a loose lead, and couldn't even figure out how to handle and harness it correctly. When Dennis came in for his first post-op appointment with a raging infection that swelled his tiny chest to twice its size, his drain sludgy and green (he also needed to begin his rabies shots), a few of the staff had some under-their-breath conversations in the hallway to discuss what needed to be done.

3:12

Tracy and her mother had had a regular date now for the past few Thursdays. After her volunteer hours at the library, her mother would stop over for a late lunch, and they'd enjoy an afternoon of talk. The next week Tracy would be back at work, so this was the last of their dates for a while. They hadn't spent this much time together since Tracy was still living at home. She'd walked her mother around the backyard, proud of her fence and her gardens. She'd pointed out the amaryllis that had bloomed this year, coming straight out of the ground on their tall stalks, leafless, with their showy, pink blooms. Her mother remembered them from when she was little, said her parents had had them. When Tracy mentioned that they hadn't bloomed last year, she told her daughter that they were biennials.

"But what did you call them, dear?"

"Naked Lady amaryllis," Tracy answered.

"Oh, Tracy," her mother sighed, "you've always been so irreverent. We called them "Resurrection flowers."

Her mother met Deb and thought she was a "hoot." Deb invited her mother to stop back over some evening for a girl's night.

"And what night is that?" her mother asked.

"Every night," Deb answered.

Over the course of their lunches, Tracy had learned the story of how her parents met (set up by friends); that before she and Aaron had been born her mother had had a miscarriage; that her mother would be shifting from a volunteer at the library to a part-time employee this fall (Monday and Friday afternoons working at the check-out desk and repairing books), and that her mother very much wanted to spend more time with her and the dogs, her father be damned.

Her mother spent a fair amount of time damning her father, and this was a surprise to Tracy, too. It seemed that his behavior after Aaron had died had been some sort of final straw. First, when he'd told "that man" (Sam) to just dispose of Aaron's things without even consulting her, and then when he'd left Tracy out there all alone because he was "uncomfortable."

Tracy enjoyed this new version of her mother: the mother whose grief had awakened her, who had some anger and fight in her. After a tirade about her father, her mother would sometimes pace, and the dogs followed her, appeasement-wagging. She'd bend down, petting each one in turn, baby-talking.

"Don't worry, dears, I won't be leaving Tracy's father, but it's high time he sees me as my own person, not some extension of him."

Tracy laughed at these moments. Despite her mother's show of anger, she suspected that her parents were probably happier now, with a little energy back between them, rather than so much distance, so much handling of each other with kid-gloves.

It was after one of these bursts of anger that her mother and Stella had first bonded. She'd been sitting, explaining about the aftermath of the Idaho trip, when she'd teared up and said, "Damn him!" not for the first time, but yelled it and said "Aaron was my son!"

At the mention of Aaron's name, Stella crossed the boundary into the kitchen. Before Tracy could make any noise at all, any small correction, Stella was there, head in her mother's lap, singing.

"Oh you big, awful dog," she said to the rather large dog invading her space. "I know, I miss him, too." Since then, they'd eaten either outside, or at the coffee table, the dogs curled around her fashionable and slight mother, who fed them crusts of bread and let them lick her fingers for dregs of mayonnaise or butter.

This Thursday, Tracy had made sandwiches of cucumber and dill and sour cream, a salad of tomato, mozzarella and basil, and a pitcher of iced tea, still inspired by her dinner at Lucy and Carla's. She was telling her mother about her visit. Her mother was always asking after Lucy, one of her favorite people from the library, and was still very curious and slightly scandalized that Tracy was friends with a lesbian couple. Despite Tracy's suspicion that both her parents had probably voted Republican all their lives, this brush with an *alternative* lifestyle seemed to make her mother feel downright progressive. She insisted on referring to Carla as Lucy's "lady friend." Tracy had just corrected her when someone knocked on the door.

All the dogs re-directed their attention from the plates of food on the low coffee table to the screened door, Smoke and Red barking, their thin tails whipping back and forth as the women grabbed their glasses to save them from shattering in contact with the floor. Stella growled. Tracy grabbed the big dog's collar. "Just a minute..."

She pulled Stella toward the hallway, called the pits.

"Mom? Can you see who it is? I'm going to put the dogs out back."

She was maneuvering Stella, who was putting up more fight than usual since someone crossed the first barrier of the porch gate, but she couldn't make out who was on the other side of the door. As she shooed the pits out, and shoved Stella, pulling the back screen door shut behind her, she could hear her mother talking low, "No, no you'll just have to wait for my daughter. Young man..." her mother's volume rising. Just as she turned back to see who it was, Stella barked.

Tracy had never heard Stella bark before and it startled her. It was broad and deep, throaty and menacing. She stopped and turned back to look at the dog. Stella was centered in the screen of the door, staring beyond her at whoever was at the door, growling low and steady. She let loose a string of barks, drool flying, and Tracy couldn't help it, she startled again, her heart beating fast. When she turned back to the front door, she could see her mother trying to hold the handle, as Greg pulled the door open and walked in.

"Tracy, I know this probably isn't a good time, but I need to talk to you and you..." Greg was walking toward her in a rush, brushing past her mother, who stood at the door, open-mouthed.

Behind her, Tracy could hear Stella barking steadily, the sound rising in volume and pitch. She was afraid she was going to go through the screen door. Lucy's words flashed through her mind, about Stella protecting her, about Stella being dangerous. That screen was no match for Stella. Tracy tried to make her voice calm.

Over her shoulder, she held up one finger toward the dog, the *Wait* sign. "Leave it, Stella." The dog quieted her barking for a moment, but kept up her low growl.

Tracy took a deep breath. "Greg, I'll talk to you, but if you keep walking toward me my dog will attack. Stop." She said all this to him in her best approximation of Lucy's low, steady talk voice. Greg stopped where he was, mid-room. Her mother still stood by the door, one hand out, as if she was still holding the doorknob tight. Tracy glanced over her shoulder at Stella, gave her a second *Wait* command. Smoke and Red were lined up slightly behind her, stiff-legged, their tails straight up and not wagging.

"OK, let's go out to the porch. OK?"

"OK," he said.

On the porch, Tracy let Greg talk for a minute or two, about how he was sorry, that he just wanted to talk to her, that he just needed her to listen. Her mother stood at the door, and Tracy could see that she had the phone in her hand. Across the street, trucks and cars stopped to fill up their tanks or pick up beer and cigarettes, slices of pizza, and coffee. As Tracy was trying to keep Greg calm, she was thinking about the dogs in the backyard, hoping they wouldn't go over the fence. She tried to maneuver Greg in front of the door, so the dogs could see them through the house, and she could see the dogs. As long as she could see Stella's big muzzle, she thought they were probably all right.

She let Greg say his piece, then she told him there was nothing for them to talk about. She asked him to leave and told him not to come back again. She told him that her mother was calling the police (at this point she nodded at her mother), and that if he didn't leave her property right now, she'd have him arrested. She told him that if he left right now, she wouldn't call the police and everything would be OK, but he was never to come over and bother her again. She didn't want to talk to him again. After she said this, he squinted at her a long time, silent, as if he were trying to figure out if she was serious. Then he walked away from her, down the front porch steps and across the road, his shoulders slumped, looking defeated.

It took a while for Tracy to calm down after that, and even longer for her mother to calm down. She wanted to call the police anyway, but Tracy told her she'd handle it. Tracy let the dogs in and they went right for the front door, sniffing all over the house where Greg had walked, all along the door frames. Tracy let Stella out on the front porch so she could inspect that too, and be sure the danger was gone. The dog stared hard across the street. When she let the big dog back in, Stella buried her face in Tracy's lap, leaning her full weight against her, and Tracy let her, petting the big dog down her sides, massaging her neck skin, the folds around her jowls.

Before her mother left, she fed the dogs the rest of their lunch, telling Tracy how much that worried her.

"Oh Mom, you're not going to give me some speech about it being dangerous for me to live alone, are you?"

"No, Tracy, not with those dogs," her mother said sadly. "Those are some very good dogs." Her mother didn't know the half of it.

Greg went to his car, parked in the little lot behind the gas station, and sat there for the forty-five minutes it took for Tracy's mother to leave. He could just see a sliver of her driveway from his vantage point. Tracy still hadn't listened to him. He hadn't realized that she had company, and should have known that that wasn't the right environment for him to make his speech. How could he talk about the year before, the year when she'd sneak out of bed, and how that other woman was just sex, with her mother there, listening to every word? He'd go back now, now that she was alone. And he'd wait outside, not ambush her in her house. He knew that that too, had been an amateur move – that she'd felt trapped, when really he just wanted her to listen. She'd started to listen a little, when they'd been outside on the porch. He'd wait by her car, in the driveway, so they could really talk – away from the dogs, with no one to hear but each other.

The dogs were out in the yard and Tracy was rinsing the dishes and putting them in the dishwasher. The phone rang – it was Cal. She thought about telling him what had happened, but it seemed such a long story, and she wasn't quite sure how she would tell it anyway. After she hung up, she looked in the freezer and was thankful there was a pizza, opened the fridge and took out a beer, opened that. The clock on the stove said 3:12, but she really needed that beer. As she brought it to her lips, the dogs started barking again. All three dogs.

She rushed out the back porch door in time to see Greg (who had been leaning against the side of her car) quickly stand upright and start backing down the driveway toward the street. The flash of rust color she'd seen was Stella going over the fence. Deb was in her backyard, wearing her sun hat, and stood up, shading her eyes in the direction of Tracy's house.

"Everything OK?" she yelled.

"No! Call the police!" And as she saw Deb running for her house, Tracy was running back through her house, out to the front. As she made it onto the front porch, she saw Greg begin walking backward across the street, waving his arms to signal the traffic to slow down. The speed limit was only twenty-five here, in the heart of town, and the cars quickly decelerated. Stella was a few feet behind Greg, head lowered, shoulders forward, walking slowly. Even from the porch, Tracy could hear the slow, steady growl.

Cars were honking. A semi's brakes screeched, as it came to a full stop at this slow-motion parade of man and dog crossing the street.

Tracy caught up to Stella, tried to grab her collar, but Stella was like a block of concrete, all tensed muscle and didn't even seem to register the woman walking next to her. She was drooling and frothing like Tracy had never seen her. Greg was saying, "Please, please Tracy, call off the dog" in a high-pitched, squeaky voice, but Tracy couldn't seem to break Stella's concentration. All around them was a burble of voices, car horns, slamming doors. Greg just kept walking backwards and Stella kept her same steady pace, backing him up.

Inside the gas station, Luke had been buying a couple of quick hamburgers and a four-pack of PBR tallboys when he heard the car horns and a semi's jake brakes.

"What the hell?" the cashier said, turning to look out the window. When Luke caught what the teenaged clerk was looking at, he left everything at the counter (including his wallet), and rushed out the door. He stood with the group of spectators that had congregated at the door, but when the awkward trio started to bend and turn around the corner of the building, he broke free and came alongside Tracy, keeping about five feet of distance.

"Tracy?" he asked, trying to get her attention. She turned her head toward him. "Is everything OK?" Stella's eyes flicked toward Luke, then went back to Greg, sweating and shambling, still moving backward, occasionally stumbling, making another quarter-turn towards the back lot, hands still up as if someone had a gun on him.

"I don't know," she answered, although she was relieved that all they were doing was walking. As of yet, there didn't seem to be any bites or any blood. She suspected that the stain going down the front of Greg's jeans was urine, and she had no idea where they were going. Once they turned the corner though, she saw Greg's truck.

He kept backing up until he touched it with his shoulder blades, and this seemed to startle him, maybe because it was hot from the sun, or maybe he'd forgotten that it was there. Stella stopped too, and her growl got louder and deeper.

"Uh, Trace?" he said, and now his voice was a whimper.

"I suggest you get in your truck," she said and Stella barked, as if punctuating Tracy's directive. Greg and Luke both jumped. Greg reached out his right hand, blindly groping for the handle, and when he found it, he gently opened the door, and moved ever so slowly to get in, inching up first his right leg, then his left, and sliding in. When he slammed the door shut, Stella charged, barking and flecking drool against the window, jumping up so her teeth were within inches of Greg's face. Inside the cab, Greg broke down, put his head on the steering wheel and sobbed. Sirens approached.

Might as Well

Cal and Tracy were in the backyard. Deborah and Luke had left awhile ago, after the police officers, after the recounting and the questions and the explanations. Greg was probably free by now, but would be charged with stalking, and had been informed that, likely, a temporary restraining order would be filed. He was strongly urged to stay far away from Tracy's residence, and the gas station across the street. The officer who arrived at the gas station had followed the small crowd around to the back lot, where he found Greg in the truck, what appeared to be a vicious dog pinning the door closed, and Tracy and Luke yelling and waving their arms as he approached, his service weapon drawn on the dog. Tracy ran up to the dog, wrapping her arms and body around the large animal. Luke, who knew the officer from high school, called him by his high school nickname "Fleet" (from his all-state days on the track team), breaking the rookie's focus and de-escalating the tension. Luke ran back across the street for a leash for Stella and everyone survived.

In the course of interviews with Greg, a few more details came out, which Officer 'Fleet' then shared with Tracy, as she sat with Cal (Luke had called him) and Deb, who'd waited in the backyard, calming the dogs and shepherding them inside, as people came in and out of Tracy's perimeter for much of the afternoon. Greg let slip that he'd met Tracy's dogs before.

"Had Mr. Greenway," the officer asked, "been over before today?"

"No," Tracy said, "not that I know of." And then she thought of Stella's nighttime pacing, her checking of the back windows, the noise she made to alert Tracy to danger. "Maybe," she hesitated, "but not that I knew of."

"Do you remember that morning the gate was open?" Cal said, standing nearby, feeling useless. She did. They'd both been sure that it was shut the night before. The dogs had been out one last time before bed, the gate secure; the gate the dogs were always intent on, sniffing it up and down, concentrating on the handle.

"Had you had any problematic interactions with Mr. Greenway leading up to today?"

"Problematic?"

"Anything that concerned you?"

"I hadn't seen him in almost two years until today. Or until last Friday. That was uncomfortable, but..." she looked at Cal, who was looking at the ground.

"I saw him, a couple of weeks ago, and he said something problematic." Tracy kept looking at him.

"What?" Tracy asked, her voice calm.

"I ran into him at Salty's," Cal said, not answering her question.

"What?" she asked again, her voice tinged with anger.

"I don't want to say."

After getting the police report and filing the temporary restraining order, after calling her mother and telling her what happened, after hearing that she already knew, because the police had called her to get her statement about Greg's initial visit, Tracy called Cal to ask him to spend Saturday with her. She picked him up and they stopped by her parents'. Her mother was in the kitchen, eating grapes by the handful, still in her bathrobe.

"Tracy, good morning!" She sounded surprised.

"Hi, Mom," she smiled as her mother tightened her robe. "This is Cal."

"Well, hello Cal. So nice to meet you!" Cal came around and put out his hand, but she brushed it aside, and gave him a careful hug, holding her chest apart from him. "I'm sorry Tracy's father isn't here. Golf."

"We thought we'd take the boat out. That OK?"

"Of course, but you'll have to check the gas. There should be some in the boathouse." She stopped to wash her hands. "Would you two like something to eat or...?"

"That's OK, Mom. We'll see you later," and Tracy kissed her on the cheek.

The lake was a little quieter than last Saturday, probably due to a forecast of possible storms in the afternoon. The boat was quieter without Deena. Instead of motoring around the lake, they headed over to the far side, where there was a nature preserve and the land was restricted from development. There was a rope swing that hung from an overhanging tree, and the water was shallow enough to set the anchor, as long as they kept an eye on the boat. When Cal asked what happened if they got caught, Tracy smiled, and told him they'd just head out. The land trust was owned by a group of rich Baptists and she didn't think they were a particularly angry or dangerous bunch.

Cal could see a few paths through the woods, and here and there a bench set perfectly in a clearing of trees to catch the lake view unobstructed. The cove ended in a tangle of roots, inaccessible.

This time spent on the lake couldn't have been more of a contrast for Cal. There was no concern about who lived where, how much the houses cost, and whether the gardener spoke Spanish or English. Tracy didn't need to check her watch to ensure the boat was back in time, that they didn't get charged extra. Mostly they used the boat like a raft, jumping off and swimming as they pleased, wrestling and playing like kids. Without Deena's watchful eye, they didn't need to pretend to be a respectable couple – not when Tracy sat astride him laughing while he was driving, and not when Cal found her underneath the boat, lit in the pale green water. He slid his hand up her thigh, hooking his thumb under the fabric of her bikini bottom, slowly circling until it found its way inside her, while jet skis circled the boat above the surface, their riders wondering aloud who was driving.

When they got off the lake, they stopped by Tracy's and walked the dogs together. Cal hesitated for a moment when Tracy offered him his choice of leashes, chose the tandem pair used for Smoke and Red. They did the short loop of four blocks and, other than Stella walking exactly between him and Tracy the whole time, it felt companionable. He finally told Tracy what Greg had said that day, felt her bristle. He apologized for not telling her sooner.

"It's all right," she said. "I understand why you didn't."

The dogs were happy with their walk and, once fed, settled down. Tracy showered first, and Cal walked around the backyard, looking up and down the fence: the gate where Greg must have let himself in, the backyard where he must have stood and watched Tracy, watched the two of them, maybe. Up by the house, Cal found several Red-sized holes dug next to the foundation – something he'd need to tell Tracy about. The large curves in the middle of the fence panels were gentle and where they dipped, they were still about four and a half feet high. Stella had cleared that easily. As much as he and Stella hadn't warmed to each other, and maybe never would, he was thankful for that dog.

"Your turn." Tracy called out the screen door. "I'll be in my room."

"OK," he said, mounting the steps.

"I'll put the dogs out here," she said, holding the door open, one towel wrapped around her and tucked at her cleavage, a second wrapped around her head, piled high. Cal looked over his shoulder, scanning the driveway.

"The dogs are fine," he said.

"OK," Tracy smiled, pulling up her towel. "I'll be quick."

When she came out of her bedroom, she was wearing a dress. It was her only one – the only one that fit well anyway. Her skin was a little pinked from the day in the sun; they'd stayed out all afternoon. It had clouded up but no rain fell. She was wearing the sandals with the little heel, and a gold chain that made her summer-brown skin shimmer. She could still hear Cal in the bathroom, blowing his nose, and quickly shooed Stella away when she approached, a single strand of drool at the ready. Smoke and Red raised their heads from the couch for a moment, looked at her, then lowered them back to their respective pillows.

"Thanks girls," she said under her breath. "I'm trying here."

When Cal came out of the bathroom, he said nothing, but she could tell he was impressed, or maybe just surprised.

"I thought we'd go to Thrasher's for dinner," she said.

"I'm underdressed then," he said, looking down at his jeans, his t-shirt.

"You look great," she said. And he did. Cal got better looking the more time she spent with him. With the little bit of sun from today, and the memory of under the boat, the sharp reflection off the aluminum pontoon illuminating his pleasure as he gave her hers, it was all she could do to gather her things and get ready to leave the house; she wanted to stay in. In the end, Cal insisted they stop at his place so he could get a jacket. He looked even better.

Thrasher's Supper Club was an institution on the lake, an old-timer's place from way back. That was part of its charm. The menu hadn't really changed in fifty years. The salmon was cooked pink-white all the way through, and served with a sour cream and dill sauce. The trout was crusted with a heavy layer of almonds. Steaks covered the entire dinner plate, and were usually cooked medium-well, even if ordered medium-rare. The only greens were iceberg topped with a crinkle-cut carrot.

Thrasher's had been rumored to be mob-connected during Prohibition, when Capone ran liquor through Wisconsin, a conduit that began in Chicago, stopped in Lake Geneva, then headed north all the way to Hurley. This still provided it with a certain panache, and the bartenders made a big show of hand-muddling the fruits for the Old Fashioneds served at the vinyl-upholstered bar.

When Cal and Tracy got to the bar, Tracy's mother was sitting at the far end, sipping white wine. The light from the early evening sun glanced through the picture windows overlooking the lake, and caught the grey in her hair. She brightened at the sight of the two of them and waved them over.

"Twice in one day," she gushed. "Here, Cal, sit next to me, and Tracy, you sit on the other side of him so that your father won't be able to bother the nice, young man." Her eyes twinkled. A snifter of cognac waited on its own bar napkin on the other side of her. Tracy could see her father exiting the men's room.

"We just finished our dinner," her mother continued. "Early birds."

Tracy put her name in at the bar. She tried to deflect her father's questions about the situation with Greg and when he kept asking, she told him they'd talk about it another time. He turned to Cal, asked him his last name, what he did for a living, and other 'checking-out-the-boyfriend' type questions.

Her mother interrupted him. "Did you enjoy the lake?"

"We did," Cal answered. "Beautiful."

"You know," Tracy's father began, "we were sitting on the dock the other day, and some local buffoon mooned us."

"Now, dear," her mother interrupted again, "you don't know that they were local."

"Aren't you a local, Dad?" Tracy asked. Her father looked genuinely surprised and stopped to consider the question.

"Well, you know what I meant."

"I do, Dad."

The bartender stopped over to tell them their table was ready. As Tracy was reaching for her purse, she saw her father notice that she was wearing a dress, and raised his eyebrows at her. He turned to Cal.

"Are you the one working on the Steinfeltz's house?"

"Yes, I am," Cal answered, pausing in their exit.

"Beautiful stonework," her father said.

"It is," Cal said. "Nice meeting you."

"You, too," and they shook hands.

After dinner, they went back to Cal's and he thought he could still smell the lake on Tracy's skin, the sun, soap, and maybe a little sunscreen, or after-sun lotion. He lifted her dress over her raised arms in the kitchen, and lifted her onto the concrete countertops. She unbuttoned his jeans, peeled the jeans and his boxer shorts down until they were ringed around his ankles, peeled back the jacket and flipped the worn-soft t-shirt over his head, and left those clothes pooled on the kitchen floor. When they got to the bedroom, she didn't need to tell him to lay still, to keep his feet together. He didn't ask her what she wanted; he caught her up with one arm and flipped her over when he wanted to and the suddenness of this movement made her breath catch, introduced a moment of fear that excited her, and the first time she came – to her surprise – was when he was in her from behind. She'd never come that way before.

Later, after they were both done, sated and sweaty, Cal was tracing between her fingers with his own. They were both breathing deeply, their respirations slowly returning to normal when Tracy said it: "This isn't going to work, is it?"

"Are you sure you want to talk about this now?"

"Might as well," she said, as she rolled over to face him.

When Cal's mom was diagnosed the first time, he was still a teenager. There was a tumor in one breast and some involvement of the lymph nodes. She had a mastectomy and surgical removal of the nodes, followed by radiation. In addition to the anxiety and fear about his mother's health, Cal remembered being haunted by his mother's body. After her surgery, he was afraid to touch her, to hug her, to be in her proximity. Deena, a few years older and a woman, didn't seem to be bothered by all the casual mentions of "breast" that had become a normal part of their lives, but Cal felt like every conversation was a potential minefield. When his mother's cancer came back, growing new tumors on her mastectomy scar, he felt he'd been right in some way about the danger of his mother's body; that somehow, opening her up, had made her newly vulnerable. Although he'd never seen the scar, tried not to even think of what his mother's body must have looked like, he knew there was no way a body could withstand that and remain whole, inviolate, protected.

Because she'd already had radiation, that wasn't an option a second time. They removed the tumors, the additional affected lymph nodes, and began aggressive chemotherapy treatment. When the cancer progressed, recurring again in the same breast and spreading beyond the chest wall, they tried another cocktail of chemicals, then another. Recurrent cancers are difficult to treat, that's what Deena said. There is no stage five, Deena said. As his mother lost more and more weight, and nothing seemed to stall or shrink the tumors, Deena took a break from taking care of other people's children and began to stay with her mother all day, managing her palliative care. Cal learned how uselessness felt.

He would lay wide awake in his childhood room, down the hall from his parent's room where his father was, and the back bedroom, where they'd moved in a hospital bed for his mother. Not sleeping, Cal was acutely aware of being in the same space with his mother, as she was dying, just a few steps away. He tried to understand what the process of dying might feel like as he lay in his too-narrow twin, the bed he'd slept in when he was a child.

All he could imagine was that it was like the first time he flew on an airplane when they took a family vacation to Florida when he was twelve. He sat in his window seat, staring out at the banks of clouds, trying to concentrate on the feeling of miles and miles passing through his body. But he couldn't feel anything – it didn't feel any different. Maybe that's what dying felt like; like it should feel like something but it didn't.

But he was stupid because pretty soon it was clear his mother was in a lot of pain. It was Deena who decided when they needed to ask the hospice service about aggressive pain management, about liquid morphine. They sat down together on his parents' overstuffed couch with the large floral pattern and Deena had a handwritten list of questions to ask. Cal and his father didn't ask any and from the other room, they could all hear Mom's low moans, her suffering. The prescription came through and Deena administered the first dose, after leading them all in to sit with Mom for one last time, to say something to her, to tell her how much they loved her. One of the answers to Deena's careful questions had been that liquid morphine can impair thinking and speech and cause drowsiness. Once they began administering it, their mother would be less responsive. Now was the time to say what they needed to say.

Deena sat at their mother's bedside for a long time, holding her hand, talking to her about her young son and the baby on the way, telling her what a good mother she'd been, what a strong woman. Cal's father asked for privacy, so Cal and Deena shut the door and went out to the kitchen, raiding the fridge for leftovers, settling on toasted cheese sandwiches after they'd cut the mold off a block of cheddar. When it was Cal's turn, he couldn't think of anything to say. Deena kept nudging him forward, but he held onto the door frame, and could only come up with "Thanks for taking us camping. I love you." What he kept thinking about was the cicada and he knew that that wasn't the right thing to be thinking about, not the right thing to be talking about. Deena looked disappointed. After they gave her the first of the morphine, his mother stopped moaning and seemed to sleep deeply for the first time in weeks. Cal knew though that she was just beginning to die more quickly, no matter how many times Deena called it "keeping her comfortable."

The one day Deena couldn't be there (her son had an ear infection), she left Cal in charge. Cal knew this was a bad idea, but he couldn't tell Deena how frightened he was. He was twenty-two, a college graduate; he should be able to take care of his mother. His father looked so haggard from waking up and caring for her during the night. Cal wouldn't have to change her (his sister assured him), just give her morphine at two o'clock, more if she started to get restless. But Deena took longer getting back than she meant to (the pharmacy was busy and they had to special order one of the medicines), and Cal hadn't wanted to give his mother *too much*, so even though she woke again in a few hours, thrashing and muttering, he didn't give her a second dose. When Deena got back, after six, she was pissed.

"Cal!" She yelled as soon as she entered the dark hallway, where she could hear her mother's muttering. "Didn't you give her any?" Cal tried to explain about giving her the full dose at two, but when she woke again at four, he was worried that it was too early, that he didn't want to give her too much, but Deena interrupted him. "Too much?" she sounded incredulous.

"Well, I just..."

"What the fuck Cal?" Deena never said "fuck."

"What if I gave her too much and she died?" Deena let her arms fall to her side for just a moment. For just a moment, she let it show how tired she was. Her pregnancy was really showing by then, and she'd been running around all day and she was trying to take care of her dying mother, and her brother (who was supposed to be the smart one) had just asked the stupidest question she'd ever heard. She looked at him for what felt a long time before she walked back to the back bedroom.

Three days later, when his mother really was dying, her death rattle shook the whole house. Cal had heard that phrase, *death rattle*, but didn't know it was a real thing, a thing a person could hear. Deena had come out of the back bedroom and said, "It won't be long now," and then called her husband, her parents' closest friends, the hospice nurse.

Cal knew he had to stay, but he couldn't stay in the house. Even outside, on what was a cool spring day, the rattle was loud, startling birds in the bushes, a deer browsing in the side shrubs. It looked up, froze, then bolted. Cal had to do something.

He spent most of the day building a wheelchair ramp up to the house, a ramp he knew his mother would never use. But the sound of the circular saw drowned out the noise, and the concentration required to calculate angles for the curve, and to measure and plan the decreasing heights, allowed him to forget what was going on inside. Later that evening, the county coroner used the just-finished ramp for the gurney that held his mother's body when he took her away.

The problem was that Tracy didn't need him. When that thing happened with Greg, she didn't even call him – Luke did. She didn't need him to provide for her or comfort her or help her in any way. And if she didn't need him, then he couldn't be the kind of man he was trying to be; the kind of man he'd been trying to be ever since he'd chickened out when his mother was sick, unable to say one real thing to her, or to even be in the house when she died.

Greg got notice of the temporary restraining order on Saturday, with a notice of the scheduled injunction hearing the following Friday at the county courthouse. He was not to have any contact with Tracy, who alleged he had been harassing her by visiting her home on multiple occasions and engaging in threatening behavior intended to cause emotional distress. Additionally, he was alleged to have harassed her mother and another named individual, that guy she was dating. He had the right to appear at the hearing to tell his side of the story. He didn't think there was much of a point.

Restraint

In the end, Tracy got the restraining order and specified her residence, her parent's residence, and the school. With the gas station so close to her house, Greg had to go to the other side of town for gas and any last minute needs, so mostly he avoided that part of town altogether.

Because of where her parents lived, it effectively cut off the whole Primrose section by the lake, where he had six clients already. He lost his township contract for plowing. Aside from that, word about his behavior and his very public arrest spread quickly, and new mowing jobs dried up (especially around the lake, where almost everyone knew the Lufts), and around town where most people considered him an embarrassment to Spook's memory.

The teachers and administrators returned to school, and the office secretaries with them. Tracy was glad to have a shape to her day again, something to distract her for a few weeks as she got used to having more time alone, especially on the weekends.

When she and Cal were parting ways that Sunday morning, Cal'd said, "I hope we can be friends" and before he had even finished the sentence, he'd started laughing. Tracy had been blowing on her coffee and started laughing too, the moment infectious. They were downstairs at the bakery.

"I can't believe I said that," he said, shrugging. Tracy smiled. "I meant it though, really."

"I know," she took a sip of her mocha. "Me, too."

"Really?"

"Yeah. I can't think of any reason not to be."

That first Saturday of being single again, Tracy went looking for her fall jacket in the closet of the dog-free bedroom and took out the box she'd packed and carried from Aaron's cabin. Underneath the dog books she'd saved, there was an anthology of poems – she'd thumbed through it during those evenings in Idaho, and remembered marking a page of Auden; the poem with the line: *I thought that love would last forever: I was wrong.* Now that she'd lived with Aaron's death for a few months, it didn't bring her to tears anymore. She'd done a little research online, and it seemed the poem was written as satire maybe, intentionally overblown – or not. When she read it that week in Idaho, she broke down at the third stanza, felt like she'd been punched, that her legs wouldn't work. It didn't matter to her how or why the poet wrote what he did; that's one thing she remembered from her literature classes in college. To her, in that moment, it seemed the perfect description of her feelings – what grieving felt like. She'd lost her cardinal directions. Aaron had been her North, her South, her East and West. Her brother, whether she saw him regularly or not, was the invisible post around which her life was oriented. With him gone, she didn't know how to navigate anything.

When they were little, Aaron had been her shadow. Two years younger, he'd done everything she'd done. When she wanted to take ballet lessons, he did, too, even arguing that he could be the boy to lift her up. When she'd wanted sailing lessons, he'd insisted on being her official first mate. When she'd been old enough for sleep-over camp and he'd had to stay home, he'd cried himself to sleep every night until she came home. Her parents called it "reverse homesickness" and laughed, but the next year she had to stay home until he was old enough to go with her. Even then he had to be in a cabin next to hers, necessitating quite a bit of behind-the-scenes maneuvering, and (Tracy suspected) some extra payment to make these unusual arrangements.

Tracy was in high school when Aaron's neediness, his sweet vulnerability, began to morph into something else. Tracy began looking at colleges her junior year, prepping for the SAT, and her parents started regaling her with stories of their own college years, at small schools out east. They got out the old photo albums with blurry photos of girls in twinsets and knee-length skirts and boys in V-neck sweaters and slacks, all walking paths between ivy-covered, brick buildings. The more excited they got, the more withdrawn Aaron became. By the time Tracy was applying to schools, Aaron was usually late for dinner, or not hungry, retreating to his room, sullen and silent. Tracy knew what this was – summer camp all over again – but she couldn't put off college for two years to wait for Aaron. She couldn't live in a dorm room next to her quiet brother, checking on him every morning and every night, making sure he signed up for activities and picked up his sand candles and pinch pots from the Arts & Crafts cabin when they were ready.

During fall break of her freshman year, she went home with her roommate to Massachusetts to see the fall color (this is something people did there – the locals called them "leafers"). They went to Northampton and walked around the Smith campus, another school Tracy had considered. She sat in a restaurant right against the glass-fronted street, watching people walk by. She ate fried tofu in cucumber sauce, trying out veganism. This place was so different than the sleepy Wisconsin town she knew, where she and her family lived in one of the big houses on the lake and had rooms and rooms and stretches of lawn; where there was no crush of people anywhere, except in summer, when the city people came up to their summer places. When she called from her roommate's house to talk to Aaron, he wouldn't come to the phone. By the time she came home for the Christmas holiday, she couldn't believe how much he had changed.

Her mother kept up a steady string of conversation, leaving almost no pauses during their dinners, while Aaron pushed food around on the plate, his silverware making grating noises, metal against china. Her father rushed home from work, through dinner, through two after dinner drinks, to the living room to pretend to watch the evening news, and went to bed. Aaron seemed half-asleep all the time, and what Tracy could see of his face was an angry welt of acne.

Tracy had only brought a few things back from Aaron's cabin: the dogs, those three skillets that she used most days (scrubbed with salt and oiled), and this box that she'd packed away for the summer – beneath these few books were her brother's journals.

She opened the journal on top. The first entry was dated October 28 – Aaron's birthday. The heartbreaking hopefulness of this. It looked like maybe he had had a plan, too. Tracy read the first few sentences, a list of things needed; the beginning of a journey. She thumbed the pages that came after, willing herself to skim, not read. Some entries were only a few lines, some went on for pages and pages. His crabbed scrawl, writing inexorably toward his death. She closed the cover, extracted it, and the three identical black and white composition books below it from the box, took them out to the living room. She thought she'd read them, in order, on the days they were written, as Aaron had written them.

With fall coming and the late light starting to fade, Deb's visits would taper off. Once it got too cold to sit outside, they'd see each other less often, both hibernating until spring. Maybe her mother would continue to visit – Tracy didn't know. The friendship with Lucy and Carla was still new but, if her past relationships were any guide, she suspected there was an invisible threshold there, too.

Tracy didn't really have close friendships. She wouldn't say intimacy eluded her, but she didn't seek it out. Her last really close friends had been in high school, and they were a trio: another girl and a boy. They'd been inseparable for a time and then they weren't. Tracy didn't remember what precipitated the break, but she was there when it happened. There'd been some fight (she couldn't remember what about) and they were making up. The girl and boy were tangled on the couch at her house, a pile of arms and legs, all physical affection, but she got up to get something from the kitchen. She felt suffocated. Maybe they weren't crying, but their eyes were wet, and she put her hands on the kitchen counter trying to will tears, to fake it just for a moment, to be a part of all of it. It was working, but she felt false. They called to her, wanting her to join them, to be a part of the hugging and crying, the whatever-it-was that necessitated the holding. But she kept putting them off – saying she was getting a drink, or that she was "fine," that "she wasn't mad anymore," whatever, refusing to join them in the cementing of their closeness. She still got an occasional Christmas card from the girl. She reported that she and the boy were still friends. Sometimes, she wrote that he said 'Hello.'

Tracy was much better with planned affection, planned engagement – things on her terms. She opened the calendar on her phone, put a reminder on the 28th, two months from now. As if she'd need a reminder.

It was a little overcast the following day, and Tracy was glad she'd brought the jacket. Even though technically summer, late August could be so changeable. In early morning, the dew and night chill lingered. Already a few nights had dipped down to the lower fifties, and she'd added a light blanket to the end of the bed, within reach in the middle of the night. Stella crept closer and some mornings the dog's snout was half-buried under pillows. More than once, Tracy had woken in the morning with her body curved around the dog, spooning, extracting heat.

Tracy was walking Stella on the trestle trail. She saw the familiar posture of Jack up ahead, and once they were within twenty feet, Stella and Willy were off. They bounded into each ditch, disappointed that all the water was dried up, returning festooned with burrs. When they got to the little bridge over the stream that drained into the slough, low with the recent heat but still moving, both dogs descended under the wooden planks. The morning light was low and sharp through the scrub and rangy summer growth; soon everything would be shades of rust and brown and gold. The doodle came up with a half-rotted carp in her mouth, bounding away, Stella on her heels, feet muddied.

"That's good for their coats, you know," Jack said, nodding in the direction of the dogs with the fish. When Jack's dog dropped the fish to swallow a big gulp, Stella grabbed the remaining chunk and ran back towards them, tail high and waving.

When they'd first walked this trail in mid-June, just Tracy and Stella, they'd met a killdeer who did its best to distract them from its nearby nest. The trail was well-graded, a mix of peat and fine gravel, and the little shore-bird moved on its flurry of fast legs with the broken wing routine, stopping and starting until it caught Stella's attention. Stella dogtracked, her easy lope, and Tracy kept looking in the opposite direction from their little dance-parade, trying to discern the location of the nest. When they got to the curve of trail, the bird took off, its low, wide wing-span just above Stella's head. The dog had sat and watched it return back down the trail, and then they'd turned and followed the trickster bird. Stella had kept falling for it, every walk, every time; the low racing along the ground became a regular part of their walks, a predictable game.

As Tracy and Jack and the two dogs walked back to the small lot where they'd parked their cars, the trail empty of other walkers, a biker crashed out of the undergrowth and whipped past them. Usually they carefully scanned the trail, calling the dogs to hook up when a runner or biker approached, but the biker caught them unaware. Jack's dog was a jumper and Stella tended to spook around anything with wheels. Lucy had told Tracy how to de-sensitize Stella, but they hadn't worked their way up to bikes, yet. As the biker brushed by them, Tracy reached out, touching Stella's flank, and sternly called, "Leave it!" Stella whipped her head back towards Tracy.

"Good girl." She rewarded the dog with her voice, bending over to give her a rub-down. The biker jammed on his brakes, throwing gravel, as Jack's dog bounded up to him, landing its muddy paws on his white t-shirt.

"Tracy?"

It was Luke.

Epilogue: The Wedding

The following July, Lucy and Carla will have their wedding, and after much discussion, it will be both vegetarian and alcohol-free. They will hire a caterer out of Appleton, and everyone will be polite, even though a few people will mention that at luaus suckling pig is traditionally served. In typical Midwestern fashion, the most common comment overheard about the food will be, "That's different." It's what people say when they don't know what to say. The bartenders, Ian and a couple of his friends, will put plenty of umbrellas and fruit in the drinks to make them festive.

Dr. Schulz will be there, with his wife, and will be red-faced throughout most of the ceremony with a tight smile – he had no idea that Lucy was a lesbian. He will whisper the word every time he says it. When Lucy introduces him to Carla, he will give her a very hearty handshake that reminds Lucy of her father's greeting of Elsa, all those years ago. For most of the reception, Lucy's father will be sitting with Carla at the picnic table, their heads bent so close together they almost touch, as they both massage Jake's ears (the dog will enjoy all the extra attention). Dr. Larsen will be there, with his boyfriend, but Dr. Schulz will be distracted from his recent brush with the homosexual agenda and think they are just very good friends. Donna will come early to help set up; she and Sarah will decorate around the pool with inflatable palm trees, using a borrowed air compressor that upsets Goose, the border collie. When the guests arrive, Donna will bestow each with a lei and make a little off-color joke. When Tracy's mother arrives, she will decide to assist Donna, leaving her husband to wander around, checking his shoes frequently for "animal excrement."

That morning, Deb will chicken out and decide not to accompany Tracy. She will say there is no point.

"Lesbian weddings are slim pickings," but Tracy will know it has more to do with there being no bar. Deb and Peggy would have really hit it off.

Peggy will have come up for the week, still tall with no stoop, even though she's approaching seventy, her hair still red, and she'll have become a woman who wears hats. She'll stay at a bed and breakfast in town, because the vintage barn renovation isn't quite finished.

When she sees Cal out at the barn, she will nudge Carla. "Doesn't he remind you of Lorne?" Lorne, her first boyfriend, the one she shacked-up with when she left the trailer. When word got around about why Carla had been thrown out, he'd said some unkind things. Peggy'd told him it was time to go. She told Carla it was because he was always late with his portion of the bills.

"Pretty doesn't pay the rent," she'd said.

Peggy never married or had children, but Lucy's brothers had given her nieces and nephews and there was a second generation now, and a third, who will have to be shooed away from the barn by Sarah. Auntie Carla will explain that their horses had been hurt by people when they were little so they were too scared to be ridden.

"Yes, even by nice little kids," Sarah will hear Carla explain to a girl wearing a pile of leis.

When the barn is finished, Sarah will be moving in. It will have a one bedroom loft, a small sitting room with a woodstove, kitchenette, and bathroom. Cal will be admiring his work one day in late June when Lucy walks up, and catches him looking at the stonework, and looking at Sarah.

"Oh sweetie, she's not for you," she will try to say gently.

"Is she... ?"

"Like me and Carla? Is that what you were going to say?" Lucy will laugh. Cal will swallow hard, his face red. "Not quite. But she's still not for you."

"I don't understand," Cal will say.

"Most people don't," Lucy will respond, a little sadly. "But don't worry, I'll keep my eyes open. You're a catch for the right woman," and she will elbow him, gently.

"Thanks but I've already got one matchmaker working on me," he will sigh, thinking of Deena and her disappointment about Tracy.

"Too late," Lucy will smile, only a little apologetic. "I love a project."

There will be a picture from that summer, taken on Tracy's parents' boat. Her mother holds a small black poodle (her father begrudgingly agreed to this dog because of its low dander and reports that the breed didn't shed). Her mother's lips are wide open, mid-laugh, the gold of a crown showing in the darkness of her mouth. Her father sits behind the wheel, looking only mildly irritated. Tracy is on the bench seat behind them, the wind whipping her hair, which is longer and caught in her mouth as she either laughs or talks. Sitting next to her is Stella, a little grey around her muzzle. The dog's back end is on the seat, her front legs on the floor, a captain's hat askew across her broad forehead, her tongue lolling out.

Luke might have taken the picture.

Acknowledgements

I would like to thank my family, who inculcated a love of books & reading early on. My father Tom with his chapter-a-night routine. My mother Suzi who encouraged my wide-ranging reading, even when my 5th-grade teacher begged her to hide my books so I would pay attention to the planned lesson. And thank you Megan, who ensures my bookshelves continue to be well-stocked, buying each requested volume from my Wish List. A writer must feed herself with words & ideas.

I would also like to thank the many many wonderful teachers I've had along the way, in particular, Bruce Bennett, Cynthia Garrett, Catherine Burroughs, and Alan Clugston. Each of you, in your own way, demonstrated the value & power of language when I was an undergraduate, just beginning to form my sense of myself as a writer & person. You pushed me to read and write, to understand the importance of the written word, to discern the way narrative & language can both reflect & shape the world.

Thank you to Jennifer D. Sims, intrepid editor & friend – who must have read this seventeen times. You & me & some Schlitz.

To my dear friends & colleagues (too many to name, the fear of forgetting one of you is overwhelming): your support means so much. Thank you for reading my work, for enduring my excessive excitement (occasional urge to cartwheel), my shares & emailed poems and texts. Many of you have been first readers of my beginning fiction, have seen your contributions make their way into my work, have sustained my energy – thank you, thank you, thank you.

To my students: you continue to inspire me in myriad ways.

To everyone at Apprentice House, thank you for your attention and encouragement. Smoke & Red send kisses; Stella gives you an appeasement wag.

About the Author

C. Kubasta was born in a small town, an only girl with three brothers. She prefers her dogs larger than she is – right now, she makes time with a St. Bernard-Mastiff mix named Ursula. Her novella *Girling* (Brain Mill Press) explores growing up girl, and the love & rivalry between best friends. Her poetry, most recently *Of Covenants* (Whitepoint Press), takes on language and how it fails us. She lives, writes, and teaches in Wisconsin, where her work explores place (the Midwest), the body (our imperfect perfect flesh), and language (its slippages).

Find her at www.ckubasta.com. Follow her @CKubastathePoet.

www.ingramcontent.com/pod-product-compliance
Lightning Source LLC
Chambersburg PA
CBHW071134200626
46817CB00018B/2966